Demons Returning

Bella Skaja

PUBLISHED BY

MINNETONKA, MN 55305
WWW.SIGMASBOOKSHELF.COM

ALSO BY BELLA SKAJA

Demons Unfolding

To Sofia and Terra, who are all full of determination and skill.
Thank you.

Phrases Used in This Book

Eagle Spirit = the tribe's supreme being
Ashinders = the tribe's village

Chapter 1

Moon Song

It wasn't fair that Oak River got to do everything with Mother and Father, while I had to stay back and take care of Grandmother, or babysit Violet Heart and Sun Stream. I'm a human too, right? No, that's a lie; I'm twenty-five percent demon, but the only demonic features I have are my feathered wings, and they are still growing! I have no use for them anyway. Father refuses to let me fly because he says it'll delay their growth if I use them before they are fully developed. Once, I tried to use my wings to fly over the river, and Father took my wings away. That was one-hundred percent unfair!

Whatever.

I sat outside our house drawing pictures in the dirt. It was the only thing that kept me entertained while I was cooped up in our house all day. Using a sharp stick, I drew a horse running across a meadow, its beautiful mane billowing in the wind; its powerful hooves *thump, thumping* on the grassy floor. Oh, how I longed to be free like that.

I heard the door to our house open, and turned to see Violet Heart storming towards me.

"What happened?" I asked, running to her side.

"Sonny took my bracelet and he won't give it back!" Violet Heart complained.

I rolled my eyes and sighed, handing Violet Heart the stick. "I'll take care of it, Vie. Why don't you draw something while I get your bracelet back?"

Vie frowned. "I'm not five, you know."

"A pretty flower, perhaps?" I suggested, turning to go inside. To my relief, Vie nodded reluctantly and sat down, sketching in the soil.

I went inside and found Sonny lying on the couch. He was tiny compared to his brother, Flame Fall. Oh man, Flame Fall was *fine*. I would give anything to wed him, but I wasn't the only girl in the village who liked him. Astraea liked him, (and he liked her, but we won't talk about that); Dakota liked him; even the elderly woman next door found him attractive. I don't blame them; he had the most muscular arms *ever*, and his face was *gorgeous*. Sonny, on the other hand, was thin and short, and in my opinion not very strong; but he did resemble his father, Pine Frost, very strongly. They both had unnatural ice-blue eyes, the same shade of dark-brown hair, and the same dazzling white smile. Sonny was two years younger than me, fourteen. I understood looking after him, but Violet Heart? Seriously? She was fifteen!

I crossed my arms and stood in front of Sonny. He turned and smiled at me. "Hi, Moon Song. Can I help you?"

I stuck out my hand. "Give it back, and you will have no trouble with your parents tonight."

Sonny rolled his eyes, reaching under a nearby blanket and pulling out a pretty woven bracelet. "Kiss me first," he said.

"Excuse me?"

"Kiss me and I'll give you the jewelry back," Sonny repeated.

"Absolutely not!" I said, slapping Sonny on the cheek and seizing the bracelet while he yelped in pain. I ran outside, casually closing the door behind me. Vie leapt to her feet, taking the bracelet from me and tying it around her wrist. "Thanks," she said. "Sonny is such a jerk sometimes."

I laughed. "He wanted me to kiss him in exchange for the bracelet. Is that crazy or what?"

It might've been my imagination, but I thought I saw Violet Heart blush. "Want to see my flower?"

I narrowed my eyes suspiciously. "Sure."

Vie took me to the dirt patch, showing me the prettiest flower I'd ever seen. It had big lush petals and the stem curled artistically around someone's hand.

"That's beautiful!" I exclaimed. "How long did it take you to make that?"

"Not very long," Vie said, braiding her hair. "I've had a lot of practice time."

"Yeah, I bet." I pulled my vision away from the flower, looking up at the sky. The sun had begun to sink towards the horizon. "You could probably go home now if you want."

"Okay, let me get Sonny," Vie said. She went inside the house, coming out pinching Sonny's ear. "Don't *ever* take my stuff just so you can get Moon Song to kiss you, okay? She doesn't like you now, and bullying me won't change that, understand?"

Sonny nodded.

"Good. Grow up!" Vie said, letting go of Sonny's ear. She walked down the cobblestone path, heading towards her house.

Sonny looked at me, his piercing blue eyes burning into mine. "Sorry I tried to kiss you. It was stupid, and I really deserved that slap. But Violet was being really harsh; I can't feel my ear!" He rubbed his earlobe.

I laughed gently. "It's okay, just ask next time."

Sonny nodded, his cheeks turning red. "Could I kiss you, *please?*"

I rolled my eyes and pecked him on the cheek. "Happy?" I don't know why I asked that. As soon as I kissed him, Sonny looked like he'd just had a shot of adrenaline. He sprinted down the road, nearly barreling into Astraea who made her way towards me, her sister Dakota behind her.

The two girls were perfect. They both had good looks and amazing agility and hunting skills.

Astraea pushed her black, curly hair out of her face. "Today was a good day of hunting," she sighed, the sun turning her hazel eyes golden.

Dakota panted, her hair done up in a lovely braided bun, a strand of hair falling in front of her face. Her teal eyes complimented her honey-colored skin and dark hair. Seeing both girls looking so perfect after being in the forest all day made me jealous.

"You only say that because you and Flame Fall talked for what seemed like a millennia!" Dakota snapped, surprising me. Apparently Astraea felt the same way, as her eyes widened drastically. "Dakota, he was helping me fix my bow—" she began. "That broke only because you were stupid enough to swing it at a bird, and you missed and hit a tree instead."

I felt really awkward. "Um—Dakota, how was your day?"

Dakota had began to walk to her house. "Fine," she said over her shoulder.

Astraea sighed and started after her. "Sorry about that," she apologized.

I smiled and went inside, shocked to see Oak River lounging on the couch, sharpening his knife. "Hey, sis."

"Hi. Where are Mother and Father?" I asked, sitting down at our kitchen table.

"They stopped at the market to get something. I have no idea what."

I rested my head in my hands, frustration clawing my

stomach. "It's not fair that you get to spend every day with them! I'm a child too, so I deserve to have good parents!"

I felt a hand on my shoulder, and saw Oak River next to me. "I don't get to spend time with them. They escort me to the forest, then they go to a totally different part of it, leaving me alone except for the occasional company of Dakota or Flame Fall." He scowled when he said Flame Fall's name. My brother didn't like him because Flame Fall was the attractive guy in the village. In every competition, Oak River always came second, Flame Fall came in first.

"It's not just that. *You* get to use your wings, but I can't use mine," I said.

"Father said that, but he wants me to not use them when other people are around. Which is to say, *never*. Also, I tried to use them to catch a runaway deer, then Father found out and took them away."

I sighed, looking straight into Oak River's eyes. They were almost like Mother's, but green. Right now, they were full of understanding and worry. "I'm sorry, I didn't know."

"Kids! We're home!"

Father closed the door behind him as Mother took off her shoes and placed them in the wicker basket near the couch. Mother walked over to me. "What's wrong, Moon Song?"

"Nothing. I just don't get to see you guys very often, that's all," I said.

Mother nodded. "We've been busy," she agreed. "But we should be open this week, and I got you a gift!"

I perked up, looking at a package in Mother's hands. "Is that it? Can I open it now?"

Mother chuckled, her golden eyes warm. "Of course, dear." She set the present down in front of me. I gingerly unwrapped it, careful not to spill the contents.

Inside, I found a small stack of paper and a complete set of colored, charcoal pencils. "Oh thank you!" I exclaimed, throwing my arms around Mother in an embrace. "I can't wait to use them!"

Mother chuckled. "Go wash up for dinner, both of you."

"I'll make dinner tonight," Father spoke from the stove, where diced meat cooked in a pan. "My treat."

I smiled and carried my new supplies to my room.

Chapter 2

Dakota

I stormed into my house, slamming the door behind me and running straight for my room. I collapsed on my bed and buried my face into my pillow, tears streaming down my face.

"Koti?" Astraea's voice sounded from outside the door. "Come on, what's wrong?"

"Don't call me that! I'm not a child! And you know *exactly* what's wrong!" I screamed. My sister was as nosy as she was pretty. Why can't she just leave me alone for once?

"Is it Flame Fall again?"

"GO AWAY!" I sobbed.

"Astraea! If your sister wants to be left alone, leave her alone!" Father's voice sounded from the kitchen.

Astraea protested, "But—"

"Astraea!" Father warned. I heard Astraea huff and storm onto the porch.

"Dakota, let me know when you want to talk okay?" Father said from the other side of the door.

"Okay," I said, calming myself. I sat up, wiping tears from my face and removing my quiver from my back. I hung it around one of the posts at the foot of my bed, setting my bow beside it. "It's okay," I told myself, "It's not

Astraea's fault that she is shockingly pretty and has caught the attention of the most attractive guy in town—and they will probably end up together—and I'll just watch this all happen—" My voice trailed off and I broke down in sobs again. I looked out the window, hoping to divert my thoughts from Flame Fall.

But ironically, there he stood right next to our house, speaking to my sister. I wanted to scream and shout and throw my shoes at Astraea, but I just watched the inaudible conversation.

Astraea was smiling at her feet as Flame Fall spoke to her. He was *so* cute. He flipped his dark hair and ran his fingers through it. His beautiful brown eyes glistened in the fading sun, which shone behind the two, so the only thing I could see were their silhouettes. Astraea laughed. Flame Fall lifted her chin with his hand and drew her closer to him and then—they kissed.

I pulled away from the window, running out of my room and right into Mother.

"Dakota! What's wrong, honey?" she asked. It was *so* hard to lie to her.

"I'm in love with Flame Fall," I admitted.

Mother laughed, "Dakota, who isn't? Wouldn't it be wonderful if—"

"And Flame Fall and Astraea are outside making out."

"What?" Mother gasped and ran outside. I heard the shocked screams of Flame Fall and my sister, and the excited squeal of Mother.

"Just wonderful," I murmured, sitting at the table as Father dished out fresh rabbit soup. I finished my dinner before Mother and Astraea came in. Both were beaming heavily, and Astraea's face was as red as the fading sun.

"Maple Lake, guess what!" Mother shrieked.

Father sighed. "What, Ocean Lotus?" He looked

exasperated. I couldn't blame him; Mother had endless adrenaline.

"I just was on the porch, and I found Astraea, *our* Astraea, kissing Flame Fall. Flame Fall! The village knock out!" Mother flopped down in a chair next to me, breathless. At the same moment, I stood.

"That is excellent news, darling," Father replied.

"Yeah, I bet you two will be *perfect* for each other," I spat before stamping off to my room, ignoring the looks of shock on my family's face.

I slammed the door behind me and changed into my nightgown, tossing my clothes into my chest. I lit a candle on my nightstand and got under the blankets, opening a book to calm myself down. I read for a little bit, threw the book into my chest, and blew out the candle, pulling the sheets up to my chest.

A few minutes later, Astraea came into our room and collapsed on her bed and sighed heavily. I turned away from her, resisting tears.

"Oh, Dakota! Can you believe that he kissed *me*?" Astraea breathed. "*Me*, out of all people!" I heard her shuffle in bed a little. "Koti, are you asleep?"

I didn't answer. I would *never* answer to Koti. What a childish name!

"Well, goodnight then," Astraea mumbled. I heard her pull the covers over her, and then I closed my eyes.

* * *

In the morning, I got up way before I usually do. I silently slipped my day clothes on, grabbing an apple on the way out the door. The morning air was cool on my cheeks.

It's a good morning for a run, I decided, and began jogging down the cobblestone road that led into the forest.

When I turned around a tree, I barreled into someone and fell onto my back, wincing in pain.

The person I hit lent me his hand. "Sorry about that," he said.

"It's okay," I replied, wiping the dust off my legs. "Flame Fall?"

"Yeah, that's me," he chuckled. "I knew I recognized that voice." He wrapped his hands around my waist, drawing me close.

"Y-You do?" I asked nervously as he stared into my eyes.

"Astraea, don't play the fool. Come on," Flame Fall said.

Of course he thinks I'm her. It's dark, he probably can't see my features clearly, but at least he will show me affection.

Flame Fall looked handsome even in the dark when I couldn't see him very well. He drew me closer and our lips met, sending an electric shock down my back. I wrapped my arms around his neck. That was *amazing*, I thought, closing my eyes. I wish everyday was as awesome as this. I stepped back, but Flame Fall didn't pull away, and pretty soon I was backed against a tree, my whole body warm despite the freezing weather.

When Flame Fall (sadly) pulled away, we just looked at each other. I heard a twig snap behind him and saw a shocked Astraea holding a basket full of herbs. When Flame Fall turned around, Astraea dropped her basket, scattering scented leaves everywhere.

Astraea gasped. "W—What—?"

Flame Fall looked at me, then Astraea, then me again. He let go of my hand. "Dakota?"

"That's my name," I admitted sheepishly.

"Astraea—Dakota—I'm confused—Oh!" His face changed from confusion to shock to horror. "I didn't know. It was dark and I couldn't see her face."

"I can't believe that you would kiss *her*!" Astraea gestured to me like I was a big, ugly, obnoxious insect. Ouch.

"Well this is awkward," I muttered. Astraea's gaze burned into my skull.

"And *you*, you let it all happen!" Astraea screamed. "I can't believe this! My own sister betrayed me!"

"Astraea, it's not like that—" Flame Fall began, starting towards my sister. Bad idea.

"Leave me alone. I have matters to attend to," Astraea said, gathering the herbs and darting away. I stared after her. *She knows that's the opposite direction from the village right?"*

Flame Fall looked at me. "Look, I'm really sorry about all of this. I didn't mean any of it; the light just was playing tricks on my eyes and I thought—"

"—that I was Astraea," I finished. "It's fine, I guess. At least I still got to kiss you, though."

Flame Fall's eyes widened. "What?"

"That was my first kiss, Flame Fall. I've liked you for a long time too, but you only seemed interested in my sister. I didn't know that what just happened would go as far as it did. I'm sorry."

Flame Fall didn't say anything for a moment.

"We should probably leave before Astraea comes back or something like that."

"Yeah. Absolutely. Bye." I turned to leave. Flame Fall seized my wrist and pulled me around. At first I thought he would kiss me again, but his expression was full of concern. "Please, please, *please* don't tell anyone about this."

I nodded, yanking my hand from his. "That kiss—it meant nothing, right?" I asked, hoping for his denial.

"Nothing," Flame Fall confirmed.

Dang it, I thought, dragging my feet back to the village.

That night, I was looking out the window and saw Flame Fall and Astraea arguing. My sister turned to go inside our house, but Flame Fall grabbed her wrist and pulled her to face him. Astraea screamed some more and raised her other hand to strike Flame Fall's face, but he grasped her other hand and pulled her closer to him. Finally their lips met, and I saw my sister wrap her arms around Flame Fall's neck.

Glad they made out—I mean up—I corrected myself. Flame Fall pulled away, giving Astraea a kiss on her cheek and hurried home.

Chapter 3

Sonny

After Moon Song gave me a kiss, I was the happiest person in the world. The next morning, Flame Fall came home grief-struck and tired. Immediately when he walked in the door I leapt to my feet. "What happened? Did Astraea dump you? Did she call you a jerk? Because you are! How did she break the news to you? I hope it was out of the blue! That's the worst! And maybe—"

"Sonny!" Flame Fall growled.

"Sun Stream," I corrected.

"Sonny!"

"Sun Stream."

"Shut up! I don't want to talk about it!" Flame Fall yelled.

"Boys!" My mother walked into the room. "Stop arguing! Sonny, stop pestering your brother, and Flame Fall, calm down!"

I hated it when she got angry. It was *terrifying*. Her dark eyes—I can't even explain it.

"You boys get along so well with Violet Heart. Why can't you get along with each other?" mother demanded.

I shrugged. "Maybe it's because Flame Fall hates the fact that I'm better than him."

Flame Fall started towards me, his fists balled. "I swear!"

Mother's hand shot out like lightning, seizing Flame Fall's ear. Her other hand firmly gripped my left ear, her pinch sending white-hot pain up my skull. "I have had enough of you two constantly bickering!" she shrieked. "I do so much for you two, and yet *this* is how you repay me?"

"Sorry," Flame Fall and I mumbled in unison.

"Apologize again, *meaningfully*, to each other and to me," Mother said, letting go of our ears.

"I'm sorry, Flame Fall. I don't like bickering with you, and I will try to prevent it in the future," I muttered, rubbing my ear. "And I'm sorry, Mother, that Flame Fall," I paused, taking a deep breath, "and I have been fighting constantly and driving you insane."

Flame Fall narrowed his eyes hatefully. "I am also sorry, Mother, for my faults." He hesitated, and I leaned towards him, waiting for his apology. "And Sonny, I'm sorry we have been fighting." He strode away to his room (that we shared, mind you. Does he seriously think he can hide from me in there?) I started after him, but Mother stopped me. "Oh, no you don't. You, kind sir, can do the laundry. There is a basket of dirty clothes by the front door."

I sighed and dragged myself to the door, finding the basket and walking to the river. "Wash the laundry, Sonny. I'd prefer *Sun Stream*! Jeez, does Mother not care? Of course not, I'm the youngest child! Ugh!" I slammed the basket down, one of my muddy shirts spilling out. I kneeled down by the riverbed, picking up the shirt and dipping it in the running water. I watched intently as the grit and dirt were washed away.

As I continued to do my chore, I was surprised to see Violet Heart sit beside me. "Oh, don't look so surprised! We have to be home a little before dinner so we can get ready."

I stared at her, confused. "Ready for what?"

Vie wrung out a pair of pants. "Hazelnut's family is

coming over for dinner tonight. Moon Song too." She nudged my shoulder playfully.

"What was that for?" I demanded, flicking water into my sister's face, smiling as she squealed delightfully.

"Don't even try to hide it! I know you like Moon Song!" Vie said. "One could easily assume that by your reaction to her kiss and the way you blush heavily whenever she is around."

I blushed. Heavily. "So what if I like her? She obviously likes Flame Fall."

"So? He's going to end up with Astraea, which diverts Moon Song to you," Vie said, folding a shirt.

I considered it. "Yeah—"

Violet Heart stood, placing the folded clothes back in the basket. "Come on. Mother won't mind if you don't finish chores because you want to prepare for—*dinner.*"

I could tell she was about to say something about Moon Song, but I shrugged and we started home.

* * *

Violet Heart had to help me get ready for dinner, which was kind of embarrassing. She washed my hair, found a nice set of clothes for me, and rubbed scented oil in my hair (which I hated). Once she was done, Vie tidied herself up.

I waited for the guests of honor to arrive. Finally, there was a knock on the door. I opened it, and Hazelnut and Blood River entered, followed by a grim-faced Oak River and Moon Song. My eyes widened. Oh man was she beautiful! She wore a silvery-blue dress that matched her pendant, and her eyes were lined with kohl, making her silver irises stand out even more. And finally, her hair was braided with long, gorgeous eagle feathers.

I must've been staring like an idiot, because when Moon

Song saw me, she laughed quietly, closing my open mouth with her hand. "It's rude to stare, you know."

"Yeah—sorry." I pulled out a chair for her, pushing it in when she sat. "Anything to drink?" I offered.

"Sonny, there is already water on the table," Father said, sitting down. "Take a seat."

The only open chair was between Moon Song (which I didn't mind), and Oak River (which I *did* mind). That guy scares me! I reluctantly sat down. We said our prayers to Eagle Spirit and began eating.

"Desert Flower, this soup is great!" Hazelnut complemented Mother.

"Actually, Pine Frost made it," Mother corrected.

"Oh." Hazelnut glanced at Blood River. It was apparent she wasn't the best in social situations.

"Are you going to the spear-throwing competition tomorrow?" Blood River asked Father.

Oh great. Sports talk. I turned to Moon Song. "So, where did you get those feathers? They are pretty!" *Just like you,* I added mentally.

Moon Song looked shocked that I was talking to her, then removed a feather from her hair. "My mom plucked some from her wings," she said, putting the feather in my hands. I regarded it with false interest.

"Awesome." I gingerly put the feather back in her hand. "So—" My voice trailed off when I saw Violet Heart and Oak River glancing slyly at each other. I leaned towards Oak River. "I'd prefer if you *don't* make googly eyes at my sister."

Oak River glared at me. "Stop staring at mine and we'll be even," he retorted.

I huffed, catching a sharp glare from Mother across the table. *What did I do? I was just protecting my sister!* I stood, taking my empty dishes to the sink.

As I scrubbed the inside of the bowl, I heard a hissing

sound outside. Father got up, curious, and walked to the door.

The next few moments blurred together. As he opened the door, an explosion knocked the front side of our house down, sending everything flying in different directions. The table was overturned, spilling soup and water onto the floor; Hazelnut and Blood River were blasted through a window; me, Moon Song, and Oak River were sent sprawling across the room, a heavy piece of stone crashing into Moon Song's head; and I watched in horror as our house collapsed around me. Mother, Violet, and Flame Fall fell backwards out of their chairs and skidded across the floor, hitting the door to my room.

Father got the worst of it. He was blasted into the far wall with such force that it broke his neck on impact, and his body slid to the floor. I wanted to sob, but Moon Song was almost unconscious, and I still needed to prove to Oak River that I was mature enough for her. I climbed on top of Moon Song (which was weird for the both of us, so chill), and shielded her body from the splinters and stone raining down from the roof. After the worst of it had passed, I carried her out of the house (it was more like dragging, but we can leave that part out). Tucking her safely in a nearby bush, I turned to get the others. Flame Fall was carrying Violet and Mother (at the same time, but whatever), and set them next to Moon Song.

"Why do you have to be such a show-off?" I complained.

Flame Fall snarled, "I'm trying to save our family! If you had any sense, you would be doing the same!"

I looked at my feet. "I don't know what to do," I admitted. Flame Fall rested his hand on my shoulder.

"Go get Oak River out of the house." Flame Fall pointed to the giant flame. "I'll see if Astra—if Dakota's family is okay."

Of course you will, I thought bitterly. I rushed back into my flaming house, coughing as smoke filled my nostrils, eyes, and mouth. "Oak River! Oak River!" I called.

I heard a series of coughs, and followed the sound. I found Oak River trapped under a large piece of wood. Moving big things was *not* my specialty, but I locked my fingers under the wood, heaving upwards with all my might. With a little help from Oak River, I managed to free him. I hooked my arm under his and helped Oak River up. He had a massive limp, but we got him comfortable next to Moon Song and the others. I turned to retrieve Father's body, but a flaming fireball crashed into the house, exploding what was left of it. Looking at the skies, my jaw dropped.

A shriek sounded from down the road. "Demons!"

Chapter 4

Moon Song

There isn't really anything I could have done differently. Yes, I was super shocked when the house exploded, and yes, it *really* hurt when the stone hit my head.

After I woke up, I found Oak River lying next to me, unconscious. I sat up, gasping as demons flew through the village, setting fires to houses and marketplace booths. Sonny's house was a heaping pile of smoking debris. My dress was in tatters, and my wings were flickering on and off, telling me that Father was in trouble. "Father? Mother?" I called, running through the burning village. A sob welled in my throat, threatening to escape my mouth. What if they were dead?

No, don't think like that! I scolded myself. I ran through crowds of screaming people, demonic figures swooping down on them, sometimes blasting them with fire, sometimes picking them up and tossing them into the air, cackling with delight as their victims fell, screeching, into the ground or fire. I wanted to cry into Mother's dress. But she wasn't here.

"Mother!" I cried. "Mom!" I felt tears stream down my face. As I rounded a fiery tree, I crashed into Sonny.

"I'm r-r-really s-s-sorry," I stuttered. "I should be m-more c-careful."

Sonny looked shocked for a moment. I wasn't even thinking. I *needed* someone right now. I wrapped my arms around Sonny's neck and buried my face into his smoky shirt. I cried until his shirt was wet. Sonny put his arms around my shoulders. "It's going to be okay. We're going to be okay," he reassured me. I pulled away and looked into his shockingly blue eyes.

"I don't know what to do," I whimpered.

Sonny picked up a sword lying on the ground and handed it to me. "Here. Protect Oak River and Violet Heart and my mother."

I nodded. "Thanks Sun Stream. What are you going to be doing?"

"I'm going to get everyone to safety and away from the fires."

"Be safe," I told him as he ran into the screaming crowds. As I sprinted back towards my unconscious brother, a demon flew in front of me, baring its teeth. I skidded out of the way, the sword flying out of my hand, and I felt his sharp fingernails rake down my back. I wailed in pain, fear surging through me as I saw the demon brandish a knife. Suddenly, someone leapt onto the demon's back and the demon reared back in pain. Shock ran through me as the demon crumbled to the ground, dead. Sonny stood, eyes wide, a bloody knife in his hand.

"S-Sonny?" I asked. He lent me his hand, pulling me to my feet. "Th-That was really brave!"

Sonny didn't let go of my hand and pulled me through the crowds. "Don't be distracted by the people," he ordered as I choked back a sob, seeing demons fire arrows at our elders. "No," I breathed.

Sonny pulled me into the forest and up a hill. I noticed

a couple of others hiding under the roots of a massive oak. I recognized Dakota, her bow ready, crouching over Violet Heart, whose eyes were as round as moons. Dakota's expression was grim, her teal eyes burning with unusual ferocity. Dakota signalled for us to join her, and me and Sonny stumbled in beside her. I noticed that we were the only ones in the wide hollow. "Where's Oak River? And Mother and Father? And Flame Fall?" I asked, peeking between the roots again. We had a good view of the chaos from our hideout.

I saw Mother and Father fighting demons in the air. Mother had her glowing sword, Aur, in her hand, swinging at the enemy. Father hurled glowing balls of magic at the demons, turning them into two-inch-tall clay statues, which fell to the ground, shattering on impact.

Cool.

But one demon stood out from the rest, an aura of power radiating his body. He threw a silver knife at Mother, who dodged the blade, but it skimmed her chest. I watched with horror as she fell to the ground. Father rushed down to her. Mother laid on the ground, and even from this far away I could see blood welling between her fingers as she clutched her chest. Father formed a cone around him and her with his tough leathery wings. The demons ganged up on them, pelting my Father's shell with magic.

"No!" I screamed, starting to climb out of the roots. "We can't just watch them get killed! I have to—"

Dakota cupped her hand around my mouth and dragged me back into the hollow. I felt ropes being tied around my wrists and an apple was stuffed into my mouth to prevent my screaming. I was tossed to the side of the hollow, Dakota giving Sonny a stern look. "Watch her, please. Don't let her do anything stupid."

I wanted to scream at her as she drew her bowstring back and aimed at something out of my sight. Sonny crawled over to me and untied my bonds very slowly as to not draw any attention. "You can *watch* what happens. If you do anything else, I will tie you up again," he whispered into my ear.

I nodded slowly and got up onto my knees and nearly screamed. Father had massive holes in his wings, and the demons were not losing steam. Finally, my Father unfolded his wings, and for a split second, I saw Father and Mother's arms wrapped around each other, kissing, before the magic surrounded my parents in a red flash, and Mother and Father thumped to the ground, dead. I yelled and pushed past Dakota, who gasped in protest and tried to put me back in the hollow. I ran for the demons (which were about 100 feet away), but someone barrelled me over and we crashed into the ground. When I regained my thoughts, I was on my back, Flame Fall kneeling over me, his hand over my mouth. His brown eyes burned into mine. His other hand was gripping a knife. He seemed to be daring me to say something, and for a moment, I was tempted to.

Then he sheathed his knife and gestured for me to be quiet and got to his feet, releasing my mouth. He gave me his hand and pulled me to my feet. "Thank you," I began, but Flame Fall clamped his hand over my mouth again and backed me into a tree, taking out his knife again. With a flash, he spun around, throwing his blade through the air and striking the chest of a nearby demon, who promptly col-lapsed into a pile of sand. Flame Fall spun back to look at me. "I told you to not talk!" he whisper-scolded. "Next time—" he cut off, looking into the distance in awe and fright.

Violet Heart ran past us, an arrow in her hand. Flame Fall and I watched, confused, as she ran into the village. A demon had a bow ready, aiming at Violet Heart. At the same time, Desert Flower shot out of nowhere and wrapped herself in a hug around her daughter right as the demon fired. My eyes widened as the arrow ran through Desert

Flower's spine. She crumpled to the ground, Violet Heart falling with her. Both heads thumped on the burnt grass and it took me a second to realize what just happened.

The arrow had went through Desert Flower and stabbed Violet Heart. Two kills in one strike.

Tears streamed down my face as I glanced at Flame Fall. His face was slack with grief, his brown eyes dull. "Flame Fall, we have to leave!"

"I've lost everything," Flame Fall muttered. "Mother, Father, Violet—"

"Sun Stream is still alive," I told him. The demons began to gather in the skies above the village. They swarmed towards the Black Mountains, flying straight towards us.

"Sonny?" Flame Fall asked. "He's alive?"

Panic rose inside my chest. "Yes, but we have to go, now." I grabbed his hand and we ran for the hollow. When I spotted the roots, I shoved Flame Fall in, diving in after him. Dakota and Sonny were pressed against the far wall of the hollow. Oak River was between them, his skin caked with ash and his shirt blackened. He must have come in when I was outside of the hollow. I climbed into his lap, curling up like a child against his chest.

"What's happening up there?" he asked, his green eyes full of concern. "What happened to Vie? Is she okay?"

I didn't meet his eyes. I knew he liked Violet Heart and it would crush his heart if I told him that she was dead. But it would also hurt him if I didn't tell him. "She's—She's—"

Oak River's head dropped. "Violet's dead, isn't she?"

"Oak—"

"Violet is dead?" Sonny's voice rose from the other side of the hollow.

Oak River and I stared at Sonny, silence ripping through the air. Finally, I crawled over to his side. "Sonny, there was nothing we—"

"Is she dead?" Sonny demanded.

"Sun Stream," I reached my hand towards him. "There was nothing we could've done." *Except stop her from running into the village like a maniac.*

He pushed my hand away, running from the hollow and knocking Dakota over in the process. Sonny sprinted down the hill and into the smoking village. I ran after him, Flame Fall and the others at my heels. When we reached the settlement, Sonny had found Violet Heart's body and was wailing over it, her head cradled in his arms. Flame Fall signalled for Dakota and Oak River to keep watch as he and I approached Sonny. We knelt on either side of him, and I watched as tears cleaned paths through the smoke and dirt on Sonny's face. Teardrops dripped down my cheeks. Flame Fall grabbed Sonny's arm, a stern expression on his face. "Sonny, Vie is already dead and there is nothing we can do about it. The demons could come back; we need to leave!"

Sonny pulled away and hugged Vie's body closer to his chest. Her deep blue eyes that were usually full of warmth and kindness were now shattered and empty. "She was my best friend," he sobbed, his voice barely a whisper. "And you expect me to just *leave* her body here?"

Flame Fall's eyes widened at his brother's attitude. "Sonny, we need to go!"

"No!" Sonny wailed, burying his face in Violet Heart's long light-brown hair. He whispered, "Her hair smells like roses." He looked at Flame Fall. "Don't you care that she's dead?" he screamed.

Flame Fall stood. "Of course I do, Sun Stream! She was the only thing I had left besides Mother, and *you.*"

Sonny gripped Violet tighter. "I can't just leave her behind."

"Sonny, if you don't leave, you'll die too and I'll be all alone!" Flame Fall looked to me for words of encouragement.

"Sun Stream, you have to be strong. For Flame Fall. For Dakota. For *me*," I muttered into his ear. At first I thought I had made some sort of impact because Sonny stopped wailing and looked straight at me (which was extremely unsettling because of his blue eyes); but when Flame Fall tried to pull Sonny to his feet, he broke down in tears again, hugging Vie.

"I—Have–Had it!" Flame Fall growled, then hoked his hands under Sonny's arms and began dragging him towards the forest. Sonny screamed and clawed Flame Fall's knuckles with his fingers, trying to pry them off of him. "This isn't going to work," Flame Fall decided, tossing his brother over his shoulder like a sack of undersized potatoes. I waved my hand towards Dakota and Oak River, and they came to my side.

"We need to find shelter," Dakota muttered and set off towards the hill. "Oak River, bring up the rear."

My brother nodded.

As I followed Flame Fall, Sonny pounded Flame Fall's back with his fists, tears streaming down his face. "No! Violet Heart! Flame Fall, please!" he wailed. "Don't leave her, Flame Fall!"

Dakota spun around and stuffed a cloth into Sonny's mouth. "I want to stay alive, thank you very much!"

I sighed, taking one of Sonny's hands in mine. "It'll be okay. You still have us," I said wistfully.

Sonny nodded, his other hand touching my cheek. This would've been romantic except for the fact that Sonny was being carried by his older brother and he had a dirty cloth stuffed in his mouth so it looked like he had swollen cheeks. I reached my lips up to his and—

"Moon Song!" Oak River called. "What are you guys doing?"

"Nothing," I muttered, pausing to let Flame Fall get a

little ways ahead of me. I let go of Sonny's hand, sighing as Sonny's head dropped again. "Nothing at all."

"Do you—*like Sonny*?" Oak River asked, raising his eyebrow.

"No!" I answered defiantly, rushing to catch up with the others. *Maybe.*

Chapter 5

Dakota

I am going to be totally honest; I have always seen Moon Song as the prissy girl who makes everyone else do her dirty work. Ew. I am going to rewind to when Sonny ran into the village like a five-year-old having a temper tantrum. Before I start, I want to say that I don't think *everyone* in our group is annoying, just Moon Song and Sonny. I can't say Flame Fall, because he is too cute, but Oak River is about a fifty-fifty; he is attractive, but a little full of himself.

Anyway, I sighed, jogging down the hill after Moon Song and Sonny. When we reached the village, I hung back with Oak River, surveying the damage to my home.

My eyes fell on a body oddly familiar. "I'll be right back," I said to Oak River. I walked over to the body, kneeling down and brushing her beautiful brown hair out of her dull hazel eyes. In Astraea's right hand was half a wooden spear, the tip glistening in the fading firelight. In her other hand, she clasped a green pendant. The pendant I gave her for her fifteenth birthday. I grabbed it from her cold fingers and put it around my neck. I closed her eyes and crossed her arms over her chest.

I ran into the forest quickly, picking a beautiful blossoming flower and sprinting back to my sister's side, tucking the flower in her hands.

I leaned down and kissed Astraea's forehead. "I'm so sorry, my sister. I didn't want any of this to happen." A tear fell from my chin and landed on her cheek. I brushed it off of her face, getting to my feet and taking the broken spear from her side. As I walked back to Oak River, I stifled a scream as I spotted my parents' bodies. Their hands were enveloped in each other's, and Father's face was burned to the point where the skin was blackened and had peeled away to reveal pink flesh. I wanted to go mourn, but I couldn't handle any more emotional trauma, and Oak River was giving me concerned looks.

I rushed to Oak River's side. "Are you okay?" he asked me.

I nodded. "Yeah, I'm fine."

Oak River brushed tears from my cheeks with his thumbs, hooking his fingers around my neck. I looked up into his enchanting green eyes, blinking more tears from my eyelashes. "What are you—" My voice trailed off as he pulled his lips to mine. I didn't know what to do; pull away or embrace him. I didn't do either, and just rested my hands over his. This moment was—

We pulled away as Sonny let out a blood curdling screech. Moon Song was signaling to us to come over to her side. Flame Fall was trying to drag Sonny away from Violet Heart's side (which I might say was failing drastically).

"This isn't going to work," Flame Fall decided, tossing Sonny over his shoulder.

"We need to find shelter. Oak River, bring up the rear." I made my way back up the hill, gesturing for the others to follow me. As I trudged through the woods, I couldn't prevent the scene of my dead sister running through my mind; her empty hazel eyes, the charred spear tip in her hand, her ashen hair. I ran my finger over my sister's necklace, a shiver running down my spine when the cold stone touched my skin.

I'm so sorry, Astraea.

As Sonny let out another scream, I tore a piece from my dress and stuffed it in his mouth. "I would like to stay alive, thank you very much."

I glanced back and saw Moon Song reaching her lips up to Sonny's. Oak River ran up to them, Moon Song stopping to converse with her brother. I sighed.

It was *so obvious* that she was going to kiss him. Wasn't it always?

But then again, it wasn't obvious that Oak River was going to kiss me. That moment was—*Weird*. I wouldn't say it was awkward, and it wasn't magical, it was just weird.

My lips still tingled from where they had touched Oak River's. But that was just a one time thing.

Right?

* * *

I ducked my head as I climbed through the roots of the massive oak. I waited until everyone had settled beside me before I spoke. "I think we should all rest tonight and discuss our plan tomorrow morning. Does anyone volunteer to keep watch until dawn?"

Moon Song raised her hand, and so did Flame Fall. I met Moon Song's silver gaze. "Flame Fall, you can keep watch until dawn, then wake me," I said. "Everyone else, get some sleep."

Moon Song glared at me, then removed the cloth from Sonny's mouth, tossing it in my direction. I gasped, ducking out of the way, but I still felt Sonny's saliva brush my cheek. Ew!

Sonny laid down, Moon Song curling up beside him. I saw Oak River scowl and shove his way in between Sonny and Moon Song. Sonny scoffed and 'accidentally' elbowed Oak River in the rib cage. I settled down near the entrance of the shelter, resting my head on my arm. Flame Fall perched on the entrance of the hollow, his silver blade glistened in the moonlight.

The hours passed, but no sleep came to me. I looked at Flame Fall, who had set his dagger down and was turning a golden ring over and over in his hands. I sat up, quietly climbing out of the hollow. "What's that?" I asked Flame Fall quietly, blinking at the ring.

Flame Fall didn't look at me. "I was going to give it to Astraea tonight."

My eyes widened. "B-But that's a wedding ring!"

Flame Fall turned his brown eyes to me. "Yes."

Realization struck me like a hard blow to the chest. I nearly fell over backwards. "You were—"

"I was going to propose to her tonight, Dakota. I was going to—" He stopped, shaking tears from his eyes. I wrapped my arm around his shoulders.

"It'll be okay," I whispered to him.

"Where will we go?" Flame Fall asked, resting his head on mine.

"I was planning for us to travel to the Southern Village and get help from them," I replied.

"That could take days! Weeks even!" Flame Fall exclaimed.

I nodded. "And there are no other people I'd rather travel with." *Except Violet Heart and Astraea.*

Flame Fall took my hand and slipped the ring on my middle finger. "Gold complements your skin," he observed. My face heated up.

"Yeah." I took the ring off of my finger and pulled a thread from my dress, lacing it through the golden ring. I tied the thread together and placed the makeshift necklace around Flame Fall's (muscular) neck. "It looks better on you," I said.

"I'm tired and I'm going to go to sleep. Goodnight." Before I could return to the hollow, Flame Fall grabbed the pendant around my neck.

"This—This is Astraea's," Flame Fall breathed. He looked at me, sadness clouding his eyes. "Dakota, I'm so sorry about her. She died bravely though; protecting the children of our village. The demons thought she was a toy and were tossing her around like a doll. One started carrying her towards the Black Mountains and my instincts kicked in. I shot the demon down, but Astraea fell and—" He broke off, brushing tears from his eyes and fumbling with the golden ring. "I'm sorry. It's all my fault."

I patted his back. "Don't be so hard on yourself. We have all lost someone and we all blame ourselves, but we shouldn't be burdened with the faults of the past, but look forward to the success of the future."

Flame Fall looked back at me. "Where did you hear that?"

I shrugged. "I guess I'm just naturally good at inspirational speeches."

Flame Fall chuckled. "I guess you are." He patted my shoulder. "Goodnight, Dakota."

I blushed, hiding it by settling back down to rest. "'Night, Sparky."

"Was that supposed to be a nickname?" Flame Fall laughed quietly.

I rolled my eyes, turning away from him. "It was, it *is*, and goodnight."

I could hear Flame Fall mutter, "I'm never answering to Sparky," behind me. My eyes widened when I saw a pair of glowing silver eyes glaring at me from the darkness. Moon Song really liked Flame Fall, I could tell. But she also had a thing for Sonny, so that meant she had two options whereas I only had one. Problem solved. She got Sonny and I got Flame Fall.

"Pay more attention to his brother," I whispered loud enough for only her to hear. The eyes narrowed then disappeared. I closed my eyes, satisfaction seeping into me. Flame Fall was *mine*.

Chapter 6

Sonny

In the morning I woke to Moon Song curled up in the crook of my arm. She clutched her silver-blue pendant in her hand. I smiled at her, and shock filled me as a hand seized the collar of my shirt and pulled me out of the hollow. I gasped and clawed the hand, relief washing over me as I spun around. Oak River glared down at me, his eyes like evil emeralds. "Stay away from my sister, you urchin. I don't need you stealing her heart only to break it," he growled.

"Oak River, no need to be jealous of *these*." I flexed my non-existent muscles. "When, not if, I take your lovely sister's heart, she will be practically *begging* me to take it. No need for me to *steal* anything."

Oak River rolled his eyes.

"Sure big shot!" I mimicked Oak River, licking my palm and slicking back my hair. I pointed at him, winking and clicking my tongue. Oak River sighed and went to talk to Dakota, who sat nearby sharpening her knife. Of course, typical Dakota. Always trying to play cool and be the hero because of Flame Fall.

Speaking of the devil, Flame Fall sat slumped against the entrance, snoring softly. Smiling slyly, I picked up a goose feather and crept up to my brother's side, brushing the soft tip against Flame Fall's nostrils. I leapt out of the way.

With a start, Flame Fall woke, batting furiously at nothing. "Get off! Get off! Ambush!" He jumped to his feet, swinging hysterically at the air.

Dakota sprang to her feet, brandishing her knife, then she and Oak River rushed to Flame Fall's side. Moon Song stumbled out of the tree, her bed head on a level ten. She looked around, her silver eyes full of fear. "What's happening? Who is attacking? Get away!"

Dakota looked around. "Flame Fall, where *is* the ambush?"

Flame Fall looked around, confusion sparking in his eyes. "I don't know, what—"

He paused, and everyone turned their eyes on me. I smiled back slyly. "Hey guys! Um—I mean it was just a feather, right? Ha ha—ha?" I looked at Moon Song for help, who just shrugged and began grooming her hair.

Flame Fall advanced on me, his eyes blazing. "Why you little—"

"Speaking of little, we don't have a ton of supplies. Anyone know where to find some resources?" I asked, going to observe some berries. "How about these?" I reached out to take one.

Dakota slapped my hand away. "Those are nightshade berries, idiot."

"So?"

"They are extremely poisonous."

"Oh."

"But I do know of a place where we can get weapons and clothes," Dakota said to the group. "Get your stuff and follow me."

Everyone followed her as she walked deeper into the woods. I was so certain that this girl had gotten us lost when the trees thinned out to reveal a clearing that held a freshwater spring. I grinned, taking off my shirt and tossing it into Flame Fall's face, and kicked off my shoes, which hit Flame Fall in his man parts. I shrieked gleefully and sprinted for the water yelling, "I'm the chief of the world!" When I reached the edge, I (attempted) a triple backflip cannonball into the cool water (which failed and resulted in a couple of bruises, but we won't talk about that). The water felt great against my aching muscles (I know, I got a *ton* of those), and my face. When I broke the surface, Flame Fall and Oak River stood, drenched, glaring at me.

"Sorry, guys. I can't help it if I'm awesome," I said. "You shouldn't be so jealous, it's not—"

Moon Song ran past the boys, squealing with joy, and jumped into the water beside me. Oak River started to go after her, then thought better of it. "I've never liked the water!"

He screamed as Dakota shoved him into the water from behind, and her laugh was abruptly cut off as Flame Fall picked her up and tossed her in the water. I reached up and grabbed my brother's hand, pulling him into the spring. For a couple of minutes, everything seemed to be forgotten: the demons, the deaths, and the severe lack of resources.

Moon Song tackled me from behind and we went underwater. I spun around and looked at her. Gods, she was beautiful. Her silver eyes glistened underwater, and her dark hair floated around her head, making her look like the prettiest mermaid I've ever seen. She smiled at me, and I don't remember if I smiled back or if I made an attempt at smiling, but I looked like a stupid idiot.

When we broke the surface, Oak River and Dakota had gotten out and were quietly conversing. Flame Fall had his feet swinging in the water, his gaze distant. I climbed out, Moon Song right behind me.

"If you guys are discussing something other than romance,

you should share it with the group!" I called to Oak River and Dakota, who both glared at me and walked over to us.

"I've found the chest—" Dakota started.

"Chest?" I asked.

"The *resources*," Dakota spat. "I can retrieve them quickly, but you guys have to promise not to do anything stupid." She looked right at me.

Flame Fall got up from the edge of the spring and walked over to the group. "I'll watch him."

Dakota nodded her thanks. "Oak—"

"I'll watch Sonny too!" Moon Song said as she wrung out her hair.

Dakota rolled her eyes, turning to Oak River. "You can help me." She walked towards the trees. I swear I saw Oak River's eyes brighten before he followed Dakota into the woods.

"Well, they're obviously in love," I murmured to my brother, who nodded slowly. Awesome. Flame Fall agrees with me for once.

* * *

Turns out the resources were two massive wooden chests that were covered in dirt. I opened the first one, the smaller of the two, and found a variety of clothing. I then moved to open the second one, but Dakota slapped my hands away and opened it herself. That chest was full to the brim with weapons and satchels. My eyes widened. "Whoa."

"Get whatever you need, but not too much so that it weighs you down," Dakota ordered.

I was the first to dig through the clothes. The others soon joined in, but I had already gotten what I needed: a clean white shirt, a leather sleeveless overcoat, clean pants, and nice boots. I set those down and went through the weapon chest. I found a small sword that was perfectly balanced when I held it in my small hands, and the leathery hilt wasn't at all scratchy when I swung the blade at nothing. I pulled a sheath out and picked up my clothes, going into the woods to change. The shirt was extremely comfortable, the pants defined my leg muscles, and the boots—well, the boots were awesome! They had tiny baby heels and the boot came up to my knees. On the other hand, the leather jacket, I could not get on. I decided that I would ask Oak Rubber, *oh, excuse me, River,* to assist me. I clipped the sheath around my waist and put the sword into it, picking up my old clothes and returning to the clearing.

Flame Fall had the exact same clothes as me, except I looked way *better* in them, and he had two swords strapped across his back in an "X". Oak River had a white shirt on like me, and leather pants, and his sleeveless overcoat was navy blue. He had a big sword strapped to his side. Dakota was braiding her hair, while she sat on a rock, her tight black pants gleaming in the sun. Moon Song wasn't in the clearing. She was probably still changing. Dakota had a bow and quiver full of arrows slung over her shoulder.

I walked up to Oak River, who was slicking back his hair. "Yo! Oak River, my man! What—"

"What do you want, mouseling?" Oak River asked.

"Okay, okay, man, chill. First, I would be a *rat* not a mouse. Second, can you help me with this jacket thingy?"

Oak River rolled his eyes and took my overcoat. He looked at the jacket. "Well, it might help if you unlaced the front." He undid the front and put it around my shoulders, lacing the leathery twine through the holes in the front and tying it in a pretty bow. "There."

"Thanks, man. I really *appreciate* it," I said sarcastically. I patted, more like punched, Oak River in the back and went to talk to Dakota. She had finished braiding her hair and was sharpening her arrows. "What do *you* need, urchin?"

I narrowed my eyes. "Why does everyone hate me?"

"You annoy the crap out of everyone and you are just—*you*." Dakota responded. "The only person here who can actually tolerate you is your girlfriend."

"My girlfriend?" I tilted my head.

Dakota face-palmed.

"Oh! You mean Moon Song? Yeah, she is not my girlfriend. I mean that would be awesome, but, but, but—" My voice trailed off as Moon Song herself appeared from the trees. "Oh Eagle Spirit."

Moon Song had a lovely white shirt on, a silver jacket thingy, leather pants and leather boots that matched the boots I had on. Her dark hair was pulled back into a tight ponytail. *Whoa.* Her pendant glistened on her chest. My eyes were widening as she walked towards me, her smile big and bright. I tried to talk, but all that came out of my mouth was drool. Finally, I got something out: "H-Hi, Moon Song."

Moon Song giggled. "You look like a rabid dog with all the foam and spit coming out of your mouth." She took the sleeve of my old shirt and wiped the spit from my face. "There we go."

Dakota rolled her eyes, walking to the center of the clearing. "Okay! Everyone! Gather around!"

Flame Fall and Oak River sat down in the grass, leaning on their elbows. I followed Moon Song and we sat. Moon Song laid down, resting her head in my lap. Dakota paced in front of us like a chief commander. "Here is the plan: we are going to travel to the Southern Tribe, which will take us a couple of days, maybe weeks," I muttered.

Dakota glared at me. "Yes, it will. When we get there, we are going to ask for their help; hospitality, if you will. It may sound crazy, but I think the only way for us to survive out here is if we join the Southern Tribe."

Chapter 7

Moon Song

I like Sonny now a lot! I found out when he jumped into the spring like a crazed maniac; and when he started drooling once I came out of the woods. I don't know if or when we are going to have a relationship, just to let you know. Also, it's official: Dakota hates my guts.

Anyway—

I bolted upright when Dakota said that we were joining the Southern Tribe. Those insects didn't even live above ground; their homes were made in tunnels beneath the valley's surface. I could *never* live like that!

The others seemed to be against it too: Flame Fall started protesting and Sonny's jaw dropped open; but Oak River just sat there looking at Dakota. He was *so* into her. I could tell.

"Dakota, we have always been loyal to Ashinders, the Northern Tribe. We can't go join our enemies just because our home is gone! That's what a coward would do, and I don't know about you, but I think that we can manage just fine out here by ourselves," I told her, twirling a long knife in my hand.

Dakota glared at me. "Who put you in charge?"

"I could ask you the same question," I retorted.

"Why don't we take a vote?" Dakota suggested.

"Wait!" Sonny said. "Before we do this, if your solution wins, but it fails, then it's onto Plan B, okay?"

Dakota rolled her eyes. "Fine, Sonny. All in favor of my plan?"

Oak River, Flame Fall and Sonny raised their hands along with Queen Butt-Pain. "Unanimous vote," Dakota said with false sympathy, looking straight at me. Her teal eyes burned into mine.

I narrowed my eyes. She could be *such* a jerk sometimes. "Fine."

"Good. It's best we travel by night. That way the demons will have a harder time seeing us," Dakota said.

Sonny raised an eyebrow. "Won't the Southern Tribe find it suspicious that five people from an enemy tribe walk into their home, armed at night?"

The corner of my mouth curled into a smile. "Yes, and with warriors as fit as Oak River and Flame Fall as well?"

Dakota gave us that 'I'll-get-you-for-that' look. "*Fine.* We will travel by daylight, but stick to the shadows. We will leave at dawn. Until then, everyone get some sleep."

"I'll keep watch," Sonny volunteered. "There is a mossy patch over there that would be good for sleeping." He pointed to the trees.

I nodded, standing up and making my way to the trees. Immediately, Oak River stood up, following me closely, and eyeing Sonny suspiciously. I elbowed my brother in the ribs. "Relax. You're treating Sonny like he might turn on us," I whispered.

Oak River shrugged. "Who knows? He might."

I scoffed and slapped him across the face. "Shut up."

Flame Fall caught up to us. "What're you guys talking about?"

I glanced at him. "You're adorable little brother."

Flame Fall raised an eyebrow. "More adorable than *me*? Stop with the lies."

Oak River glared at him. "Stop crushing on my sister and we will be even."

"He's not crushing on me. And besides, I like Sonny better anyway," I told them.

They stopped arguing and looked at me like I had grown a third eye. "*Really?*"

I nodded, pushing my way in between them. We found the clearing and got settled for the night. I had found a mossy rock and used it as a headrest, lying down near a log. I watched as the sky changed from blue to purple-red to indigo to black. Awesome.

Dakota appeared from the undergrowth, Sonny behind her. Sonny looked like Dakota had just punched him; he had a black and purple bruise on his cheek. He sat on the log, his tiny sword ready. I looked at him and he looked at me. "You okay?"

"Dakota wasn't happy that we stood up to her," Sonny muttered.

I sat up and looked around. Oak River and Flame Fall were snoring loudly, and Dakota was curled up against a tree. I pulled myself onto the log next to Sonny, resting my head on his shoulder. "I found a satchel that has a ton of medical supplies and maps in it," I told him.

"Really?" Sonny asked.

"Yeah." I put the leather purse in my lap and pulled out bandages, herbs, and a map of the valley. Sonny looked over them, unrolling the map. "Cool."

I smiled and put the supplies back into my bag. "Don't tell Dakota. She'll blow."

"Yeah," Sonny chuckled. His blue eyes glowed. A cold breeze drifted through the clearing. I shivered and moved back down to the mossy floor, Sonny moving with me.

I snuggled up against him and curled up.

"It's kind of cold," I said. *No need to state the obvious.*

Sonny wrapped his arms around my shoulders. I smiled up at him. "Moon Song," he started, "I really like you. I think you are beautiful and funny and smart and I love the way your eyes light up when you laugh."

My face grew hot and I looked up at him. Moonlight peeked through the trees, turning his brown hair copper. I brought my lips up to his, closed my eyes, and we kissed. It wasn't just any kiss. This one sent waves of warmth across my body, and my hairs stood on end. As we kissed, a balmy breeze blew away the cold, ruffling my hair. I smiled as we kissed. This was amazing.

When I pulled away, Sonny stared at me. "Wow."

I butted him affectionately. "Wow indeed." Resting my head on his chest, I closed my eyes and drifted into a peaceful sleep.

* * *

I woke suddenly. I don't know why, but when I opened my eyes, I remembered the kiss. Whoa.

I sat up, pleased to see that everyone was still asleep. The moon was still in the sky. It would probably be a few hours before the sun rose. My heart skipped a beat. Something rustled in the bushes across the clearing, right behind Flame Fall. I grabbed my knife from within my boot, wrapping my hand around Sonny's and stifled a scream when I saw a pair of glowing hazel eyes peering at me from the shadows.

A dark, brown wolf stepped into the fading moonlight. Its eyes were not crazy like a normal wild wolf, but this wolf's eyes flourished with kindness. Something about this animal was familiar, which made me uneasy. It stepped over the sleeping boys and paused to stare at Dakota for a second. It padded silently over the moss until it was a mouse-length from my face. I scrambled backwards, holding out my knife. During my panic, I stepped on Sonny's hand, startling him awake.

"Wha—?" He broke off when he saw the wolf. He stumbled to his feet and in his clumsy haste, tripped backwards over the log and landed hard on his back.

No need to be afraid, a voice said. It seemed to be coming from the wolf, but its jaws weren't open.

Moon Song, you know who I am, yes?

I blinked. A talking wolf. But now that I thought about it, the voice sounded familiar.

I sheathed my knife. "Astraea."

Chapter 8

Dakota

I was awake when the wolf entered the clearing, but I pretended to stay asleep for the sake of my safety. I heard my sister's voice and Sonny's gasp. I heard Moon Song as she spoke Astraea's name. At that moment, I rolled over, readying my bow and springing to my feet. The wolf spun around.

Sister, I am glad to see you are awake, Astraea said.

I didn't want to admit it, but it was my sister. This wolf was Astraea reincarnated.

"How come they are not awake?" I asked, gesturing to Oak River and Flame Fall.

They cannot hear me, Astraea said.

"Why not?"

"Who are you talking to? The wolf?" Sonny asked, dusting the dirt off of his pants.

I glared at Sonny, balling my fists. "Yes, Sonny, the wolf!"

"Is that sarcasm?" Sonny asked, moving to stand beside Moon Song. I saw him slip his hand around Moon Song's.

"No! Idiot!" I screamed, a little more loudly than I intended. Flame Fall sat up, rubbing his eyes. Oak River stirred, his snores stopping abruptly. Flame Fall scrambled to his feet, baring his swords. Astraea looked at him with her beautiful hazel eyes, and Flame Fall slowly lowered his swords.

Flame Fall, Astraea breathed.

Flame Fall's swords clattered to the ground and his face went slack. "It can't be."

My sister approached Flame Fall and butted his legs. She looked into the trees and let out a soft howl. A little while later, a small doe bounded from the undergrowth, leaping hysterically around the group. She ran into Sonny, who exclaimed and toppled over. The doe licked Sonny's face joyfully.

"Who is this?" I asked Astraea, watching the doe weave through Flame Fall's legs and squealing happily.

Violet Heart is still getting used to her new body, and she has been bugging me our whole journey, Astraea sighed.

Flame Fall stared at the doe—Violet Heart—in awe, and Sonny laughed jollily as Violet Heart tumbled into him again and licked his face. He wrapped his arms around her neck. "Oh, Vie, how I've missed you!"

Violet Heart said something in Deer that I couldn't understand, but Sonny seemed to have understood perfectly.

"I'm so confused," I muttered.

Astraea licked my hand. *Don't worry, I'm sure you'll figure it out.*

"Yeah. Why are you here, other than to see us?" I asked.

Even as a wolf, my sister still mastered the 'you're-such-an-idiot' look. *We are here to escort you to the Southern Tribe, even though it is a terrible idea and will most likely fail.*

"Of course." I turned to the group. "Listen up, everyone!"

Everyone looked at me, Violet Heart included.

"Astraea and Violet Heart are here to guide us to the Southern Tribe. We will leave for that in a little bit, so gather up your stuff and let's head out," I announced.

Oak River had woken up and was staring at me like

I was crazy. I gave him my 'I'll explain later, sorry for the confusion' look and followed Astraea into the forest. I heard Flame Fall sheath his swords and urge the rest of the group onward. I glanced over my shoulder and saw Oak River hurrying towards me, Sonny and Moon Song walking side-by-side behind him, their hands enveloping each other's. Flame Fall brought up the rear, his (gorgeous) face still slack with shock. His wedding ring still hung around his neck, it glinted in the rising sun, sending golden beams of light shining through the trees. Flame Fall caught me looking at him and I whipped my head to face forward again, my face hot.

Oak River reached my side, Violet Heart prancing around his legs. "I never thought I'd see her again," he whispered.

I nodded. "I understand."

"No, you don't, Dakota. This is different. I *saw* her die, I *watched* the arrow cut into her stomach, and her body hitting the ground. Besides—"

"Did you love her?" I asked, glancing sideways at Oak River, whose face had grow redder.

"What?"

"Did you love her?" I inquired. "Be honest."

"I—I—uh—um—I—I—yes," he admitted, suddenly interested in his sword hilt.

"Do you still?"

"Yes, but—"

Astraea's voice sounded from ahead, *You should quiet your conversation; Vie is picking up every word of it.*

Oak River lowered his voice. "I don't know, honestly. I think so."

I looked in front of me, examining the trees (but not really. I just wanted something to look at other than some cute boy's face). "Do you love me?" My voice was barely a whisper.

Oak River was silent as we trudged onward, so for a minute or so, the only thing I could hear was the quiet giggling of Moon Song and Sonny and the *clump, clump* of Vie's hooves on the ground.

"Dakota, I—I—" Oak River started.

"It's fine" I said, my heart feeling like an eagle was smooshing it in its talons. "That's enough of an answer for me." I approached Astraea. "I'll be right back, I need to take a breather," I told her.

Fine, but don't be long, she commanded.

I dipped my head, doubling back and stopping behind a maple tree, and collapsing onto my knees. I wanted to cry until my lungs hurt. Flame Fall, my first love, liked my sister, who died, so I thought, *Hey, maybe he will get over her and get into me!* But then, Astraea came back as a wolf, his favorite animal (don't ask how I know). Next (but wait there's more), I fall for Oak River, who I think might like me, but I'm not one-hundred percent sure, so I ask. Then he replies with stammering and stuttering, and because he didn't answer 'yes' right away, it's a 'no!' Why has Eagle Spirit cursed me to be single for life?

I didn't mean to cry, but tears rolled down my cheeks as I replayed my traumatic life through my head. I gasped, trying to control my emotions, and stood.

My heart skipped a couple beats when I felt a hand on my shoulder. I spun around, shock and relief gripped my chest when I saw Oak River's face.

I blinked. "Oak River—"

He grabbed my waist and drew me into a kiss (Note to self: Oak River is a really good kisser). I ran my hands through his hair, resting them around his neck. Since I was slightly shorter than Oak River, he lifted me into the air so we were eye-level, but he was off-balance slightly and we tumbled through the grass, laughing.

When we halted to a stop, Oak River was lying on top of me, his black hair full of grass and leaves. I chuckled and ruffled his hair, sending forest remnants fluttering to the ground. Oak River still had hold of my waist, and I wrapped my hands around his neck again, and for a couples minutes, we just laid there and made out. It was indescribable. Oak River rolled off of me, getting to his feet and lending me his hand. I took it and began dusting myself off as soon as I was balanced. "We should probably get back before the others get suspicious."

"Yeah." We started after the group. "But next time," Oak River said, "Let me finish what I was going to say."

I smiled and punched him in the shoulder, running to catch up to the others. Oak River scoffed and thundered after me. Soon we were with everyone else, both panting hard.

Astraea looked back at me. *What took you so long?* But her voice wasn't angry, more like teasing. She knew.

"How did you know?" I asked her.

Astraea snorted. *I am older and wiser than you, Dakota. I know a lot of stuff.*

"You're older, that's obvious," I commented, laughing a little.

I would not start that game with me, child.

I rolled my eyes. "Sure, sure."

Astraea laughed, that is, if wolves laughed. *Now, on a more serious level, I had some people tell me—they shall remain nameless—that you are not treating them the way you should. In other words, bullying.*

I furrowed my eyebrows and glanced backwards at Sonny and Moon Song, who both glared at me. Wow.

If you want them to treat you like a true leader—

"The alpha in your case," I corrected.

Yes, you could say that.

I felt satisfied with my nature knowledge.

But right now, I think you are acting like an omega.

I folded my arms in front of me, dropping my gaze to my feet. Omega was the lowest possible ranking of a wolf pack. Dang. Roasted by my own sister.

Astraea huffed with contentment. *Come on, Omega.* She flicked her bushy tail, brushing my face. Ugh.

I heard Flame Fall laugh behind me. "Yes, Omega, listen to your sister."

I forgot that he could hear her too. So could Moon Song, who was never going to let this blow over. Sonny and Flame Fall could hear Vie, and Oak River couldn't hear anyone as far as I was concerned. Ha.

Astraea stopped abruptly, sniffing the air. *Something is wrong. There is a disturbance in the air.*

"What's going on?" Sonny asked.

Oak River threw a dirty glare at him. "Something is wrong."

"Well that's obvious," Sonny scoffed. "Why would Astraea stop if there wasn't?"

Demons, Astraea growled. *Hurry.* She sprinted ahead. I ran after her, and the others soon got the message. Fear rose in my chest as a winged shadow obscured the sun from me. The demons had come.

Chapter 9

Sonny

I'm just going to run through the highlights. After me and Moon Song stood up to Dakota, she punched me in the face (ouch!), Moon Song and I kissed (whoa!), and when I found Violet Heart was still alive, I was the happiest boy alive. She was happy to see me too because she covered me in licks—deer kisses I assume—and rubbed her cheeks against mine.

Coming back to where we last left off—

We were just walking, you know regular walking and stuff, and then out of the blue, Vie starts going crazy and her voice sounded, *The demons! Astraea the demons!*

Astraea got the message and sprinted into the forest, Dakota at her heels. I ran after them, pulling Moon Song after me. I heard Flame Fall running behind us, and Vie stayed at my side, guiding me away from the demons.

We ran for a few minutes before coming across a large, no huge, badger hole in the side of a tiny hill. Astraea nudged Dakota into the darkness, urging Oak River after her. When we came to the entrance, Vie pushed me in, and me and Moon Song tumbled into blackness. We stopped at the bottom, and I heard Flame Fall slide in beside me. Dakota and Oak River were nearby, panting. Astraea and

Vie gracefully walked to the bottom, nothing visible except for Astraea's glowing hazel eyes and Vie's luminescent, deep blue eyes. Both animals spun around, ready to defend us.

The hole suddenly lit up, and I looked around and saw the light was coming from Moon Song and Dakota's amulets. "What in the name of Eagle Spirit is *that*?" I asked.

Moon Song wrapped her hand around her necklace and for a moment, the light was dimmed, but then the pendant glowed as bright as one-thousand suns.

All of a sudden, I heard the menacing laugh of the demons as they looked down the hole. "So much for hiding!" they cackled.

I heard Astraea growl something in Wolf. Dakota translated in a soft whisper, "She and Violet Heart will hold them off while we escape. They will catch up when they get a chance."

"*If* they get the chance," I heard Dakota mumble.

I nodded, shifting onto my feet. Astraea howled and I unsheathed Tiny (my sword) and ran after Astraea and Violet Heart, who sprinted at the demons. The others followed me closely.

As soon as we exited the den, demons surrounded us. I swung wildly at one that lunged at Moon Song and watched it turn into dust. I grabbed Moon Song's hand and we raced for the trees. Moon Song climbed up the nearest one, me following closely behind. We perched on the bough and waited for the others.

Dakota was the last one out of the den, but before she could make a break for the woods, a demon grabbed her braid and yanked her backwards. With his free hand, he unsheathed a copper knife and put it across Dakota's throat. She gasped and grasped her hair, her face scrunching up in pain.

"Oh, Black Raven would pay a pretty price for you," the

demon said. His scary, black eyes scanned over us. "He would pay us a fortune if we turn you all in."

Astraea growled and launched herself onto the demon's back, biting his neck. The demon howled, letting go of Dakota and thudding dead to the ground. Astraea growled and glared at the other demons, daring them to touch anyone. A small demon leapt at Astraea, but Violet Heart jumped into the air, kicking the demon's skull with her hooves. That fiend crumpled (unconscious) to the ground. After seeing their companions' defeat, the two remaining demons flew back to the Black Mountains. Astraea's eyes had lost all warmth and were now glittering with hostility.

Moon Song and I climbed down the tree, faced by a raging Oak River.

"Our lives were at risk and you guys *hide*?" he demanded. "What kind of bravery is that? Dakota could have died! She *would* have died if it hadn't have been for Astraea!"

Moon Song stepped in front of me. "Oak River calm down! I was scared and Sonny came with me to protect me! We didn't want to be in the way of anything, okay? Relax, for Eagle Spirit's sake, Oak River! If this is how you are going to be treating me, I don't want to journey across the valley with you. You're just as bad as those demons!" Her face was turning red, and she had her fists clenched so tightly that her knuckles were turning white. "Stop acting like my father, okay? I don't need a personal bodyguard, especially if it's *you*."

Moon Song pushed past her brother, leaving both of us in shock.

"I've never seen her get angry like that before," Oak River muttered.

I shrugged, sheathing Tiny. "To be fair, you *were* being a bit of a jerk."

Oak River's eyes turned from that soft forest green to

Evil-Overlord green. The look on his face told me I should run, so I did. I turned around and sprinted back the way we had come, pushing myself as fast as I could. I heard Oak River coming after me. *Uh oh.*

Something wrapped around my ankles and I fell onto my face, getting a mouthful of dirt.

Oak River knelt on my chest, muffling my breathing. "You have no right to love my sister! You are a player, and I don't need some mouseling like *you* going off and breaking her heart! So— let—it— go!"

With the last three words, he punched me in the face. Hard. I felt blood trickle out of my nose. Oak River grabbed my collar and pulled me to my feet. "Fight like a man!" he shouted, kneeing my guts. I doubled over, groaning. Oak River swung at my face again, but I ducked and kicked him in his man parts. Ha. Oak River huffed and kicked straight out with his foot, catching me in the stomach. My feet were lifted off the ground and I went flying. I hit the ground with a sickening *thud*, sliding across the grass and crashing into a tree.

Blood welled in my mouth and panic gripped my heart when I saw Oak River storm towards me. Suddenly, Moon Song burst out of the trees, running after Oak River. She grabbed his arm, trying to stop him. "Please don't do this, brother! Oak River please!"

"Stay out of this, Moon Song!" Oak River ordered, elbowing her to the ground. Moon Song lay there, shocked, and tried again. Oak River spun around, gripping her wrists. He picked up a long vine that he had used to trip me and tied Moon Song's hands behind her back, pushing her to the ground. I watched her struggle with her bonds.

Oak River turned back to where I was, throwing a punch into my gut. I gasped, unable to move. Oak River drew back his fists for another strike, when Flame Fall sprinted into view. "Stop messing with *my* brother. *I* am the *only* person who is allowed to do that!"

He barrelled into Oak River, punching him multiple times in the stomach. Red and black spots danced across my vision, and everything blurred and went into slow-motion. I tried to get to my feet.

Bad idea.

My legs felt like jelly, and I immediately fell to the ground, and the world around me crumbled into darkness.

"I HATE YOU!" Moon Song yelled at Oak River.

I had just woken up, but my eyes remained closed as I listened to Moon Song's conversation:

"He could die and it would be all your fault!" Moon Song screamed, her voice catching in her throat.

"He doesn't treat you right!" Oak River protested.

"How would you know a right relationship from a wrong one? You've never had a relationship yourself!" Moon Song retorted. "So don't tell me what to do!"

Oak River didn't reply to that comment. "Moon Song—"

"Shut up and get out of my life! I don't need you anymore; I'm sixteen and I don't need you anymore!"

Oak River started to say something but stopped and I heard him walk away, replaced by someone else.

"How is he?" Flame Fall asked.

"I don't know," Moon Song admitted. She sounded like she was holding back tears (of course she was; I would too if I was her). "I don't know, Flame Fall. I don't know."

"It's okay, Moon Song," Flame Fall said.

I opened my eyes and saw Flame Fall had his arms wrapped around Moon Song, who was sobbing into his shirt.

"What did I miss?" I asked. We were back in the dark hole again.

Moon Song pulled away and looked at me, gasping and throwing her cute little hands around me. I winced. "Ouch!"

Moon Song pulled away, and I saw white bandages wrapped around my torso and I felt a wet cloth on my head. I felt like crap. "What happened? Between you and Oak River I mean." I asked, trying to sit up and gasping as pain gripped my arm as I fell back down. Moon Song helped me into a sitting position. Flame Fall looked at me, his devilish smile cracking across his face.

"How are you feeling, Sonny?" he asked.

"I've had better days," I confessed. I looked at my arm and saw I had bandages wrapped thickly around my left arm. "What?"

"I'll be back," Flame Fall said, walking away.

Moon Song waited until he was out of hearing distance. "When you fell over after you went unconscious you broke your arm. I don't have the proper materials, but I fixed it up as best as I—"

I used my good hand to draw her into a kiss. She smiled, and so did I. "Moon Song?" I asked after we finished.

"Hmm?"

"Want to be my girlfriend? After we get back from all of this—"

Moon Song smiled and kissed me on the cheek. "Why wait?"

I stared at her, incredulous. "What?"

She kissed me again and gave me that 'you're-an-idiot-but-I-love-you' look. "I'll be your girlfriend now."

Chapter 10

Moon Song

After Sonny passed out, Violet Heart chewed my bonds off, and I gave Oak River a couple of well-earned punches and slaps before dragging Sonny back to the hole. Well, I made it halfway, then Astraea showed up and gave us a lift the rest of the way. She is *strong*!

Once I got Sonny settled, I unpacked my medical bag and asked Astraea to wet down a cloth. Once she returned with the soaking towelette, I cleaned off the blood from Sonny's face and torso. That required me to remove his shirt, which was kind of awkward, but at least he was knocked out. I wrapped his belly in bandages and force-fed him a couple of pain-relieving herbs. I paced anxiously around the tiny hole as I waited for Sonny to wake up. Oak River came into the hole and we argued, and after he left, my chest heaved with anger. Then Flame Fall came in and I cried into his shirt. I didn't care if he judged me or not; I needed someone conscious to cry into. When Sonny woke up, all of my worries vanished in a cloud of joy. I hugged him and Flame Fall left and we kissed and it was *awesome*! And when he asked me to be his girlfriend, I said 'yes' (DUH) and we kissed some more.

Anyway—

I stood up, lending my hand out to Sonny. "Be prepared to get vertical," I warned him.

Sonny nodded and got to his feet, instantly sitting again. "Whoa."

I smiled.

"Okay, I'm ready this time," Sonny promised and I heaved him upright. He had to lean on me, but at least he was walking. With great difficulty, we got out of the hole, and found the others waiting outside. The sky was gray and overcast. Flame Fall was talking to Astraea in Wolf, which was kind of cute; and Dakota was sharpening her arrows while glaring daggers at my brother, who was playing tag with Violet Heart. Cute again, but I'm still mad at him! Violet Heart was really fast and every time she was 'it', she would barrel into Oak River's back and knock him to the ground, doing a victory dance on his back before bouncing off again.

When Vie saw Sonny, she pranced over to him and licked his hand lovingly.

"What a good big sister," I complimented.

Violet Heart bleated happily and nodded south.

"Vie says we should get going," Sonny translated. I nodded, waiting for the rest of the group to gather around, then we set off towards the Southern Tribe.

It wasn't long before the trees thinned out to reveal the Great River; the river dividing the Southern and Northern Tribe territories. It was about twenty feet across and maybe six feet deep. The real problem was that the water was rushing by so fast that if I were to put a single foot in the water, I would've gone under within the minute. The sky was thick with rain clouds, which didn't help our problem.

Everyone looked at Astraea, who observed the water closely. *Hmm—last time we crossed this river, it was barely moving. Strange.*

Violet Heart stepped forward and squeaked something. Astraea looked back at her and nodded. *Demons did this.*

"Demons can control the Great River?" Oak River asked.

I rolled my eyes. "They can kill super magical beings like our parents and can breathe fire! Of course they can!"

My brother looked shocked at my sharp tone, but he deserved it.

Flame Fall stepped forward. "I could swim across first to see if it's safe," he suggested.

No, Astraea said firmly, *I will go first. You are more valuable alive.*

As soon she said that a hard downpour began.

I had no idea whatsoever what she meant by that, but I watched Astraea slip into the water, paddling across. Her wolf ears were perked, her muzzle lifted high as she tried to stay above water. Once she reached the opposite side, she climbed out and shook out her fur.

Violet Heart, you stay on that side until everyone gets across, okay? Astraea commanded.

Vie nodded and nudged Dakota towards the water. Dakota jumped in, her head slipping under almost instantly. Violet Heart tensed and ran to the bank, ready to jump in, when Dakota resurfaced, panting, a couple feet from the opposite side. Astraea grabbed the collar of her sister's shirt and heaved her onto the grass. Dakota sat up and coughed up water, waiting for the next victim—I mean *person* to cross.

Oak River cautiously approached the water, letting out a startled yelp as he fell into the water. I was surprised by how fluently Oak River moved in the water; he was across in no time.

That left me, Sonny, Flame Fall, and Violet.

"I'm not going until you guys get over there," Flame Fall told us stubbornly. "Especially *you.*" He poked Sonny in the stomach. I smiled as Sonny let out a small laugh.

"I'll go," I offered. I leapt into the river, gasping as the cold water seeped through my clothes, weighing me down. I swam to the riverbank on the other side, my energy draining *fast*. Relief washed over me when Astraea stuck her head an inch above the water, ready to grab my shirt. Suddenly, a piece of wood about the size of my two fists came speeding downstream and crashed into the side of Astraea's head, sending the she-wolf reeling. I cried out as I felt myself being pulled away from the bank. My hands flew out, trying to grasp something. My head went under once. Twice.

A hand flew out and grabbed hold of my arm, pulling me onto the pebbly shore.

I bent over and coughed up water. After I regained my wits, I looked to see who my rescuer was. "Dakota?"

Dakota wrung water out of her hair. "I might seem like it, but I'm not so cold-hearted that I'd let you drown."

I nodded, looking across the river. Sonny was staring at me. "Are you okay?" he called.

I smiled. "Yes, Sonny."

Sonny sighed, and after a second-long talk with Flame Fall, he slid into the water. Realization struck me hard.

Sonny had a broken arm. You can't swim with a broken arm!

Too late; Sonny's eyes widened as his head was submerged in water. He came up again, and I sighed in relief. Then he was gone, popping back up again in a few seconds. Then he went under again.

But he didn't resurface.

Panic rose in my chest. Others seemed worried too; Violet Heart tensed, crouched on the riverbank; Flame Fall looked ready to jump into the water; and Dakota watched the surface intently (Astraea was bordering unconsciousness, so she didn't have time to worry). But Oak River just sat down, watching the scene in amusement.

I stripped off my boots and bag, tossing them towards my brother (a boot hit him in the face so *ha*!).

I leapt off of the pebbles, diving into the icy water. Immediately, I was swept downstream. I opened my eyes (the water was very clear, so that helped), and began searching for Sonny. Something glinted on the riverbed, and I swam down and picked it up.

It was Tiny, Sonny's sword.

No, no, no!

I searched frantically through the river until I had to come up for air. It was then that I saw a head of dark hair a couple feet to my left.

"Son—" My cry was cut off as a surge of water went into my mouth, choking me. I gasped for breath and swam towards him, the current threatening to pull me under. I reached Sonny's side and saw his ice blue eyes were round with fear.

I hooked my arm under his and began paddling towards the shore, and saw Dakota extending her hands.

Suddenly the water sucked us under the surface, pulling us to the bottom. *We are going to die.* My feet hit the pebbled bottom, and I looked down, panic crawling up my throat as the riverbed seemed to swallow my foot. I saw that they were doing the same to Sonny. We were stuck.

Me and Sonny met each other's gaze and he slipped his hand into mine. I smiled at him. I grabbed his other hand and we pulled each other closer. Just as our lips touched, Sonny let out a muffled yelp and was rocketed upwards in a flash of air bubbles. I watched him break the surface, and I lost sight of him.

I tried to pull my foot out of the riverbed, but the pebbles were almost up to my knees, and my lungs were screaming for air.

Hearing a splash, I turned my head and saw Flame Fall

swimming towards me. When he reached my side, he yanked at my leg. No luck. He tried again, propelling himself upward. Flame Fall pulled my leg out of the pebbles, hooked his arm around my chest, and swam us to the surface.

The cold air felt warm compared to the icy water, and I took many deep breaths. Flame Fall paddled to the shore, climbing out with surprising speed and hauling me onto the waterside, dropping me once we reached the grass. Tiny clattered out of my hand.

I laid there for a second, then sat bolt upright and vomited out water. Flame Fall watched me, concerned. "Are you okay?"

I nodded, holding my stomach. "We should get to shelter."

Flame Fall nodded and helped me to my feet. I started to walk towards the trees again and stopped abruptly.

"What's wrong?" Flame Fall asked.

I spun around, shock gripping my heart when I saw him motionless on the shoreline. "Sonny."

Chapter 11

Dakota

When I saw Sonny shoot out of the water, I had a mini heart-attack. Let's rewind shall we?

After Moon Song disappeared to look for him, I knew that she had a slim chance of survival, but I let her try. Astraea laid in the grass, blood dripping from where the rock had hit her.

Oak River was on his feet now, scanning the surface. Violet Heart was running around on the opposite side, bleating like crazy, and Flame Fall had unsheathed his swords and put them on the ground. He dove into the water.

The water started bubbling a little ways down-shore, and I readied my bow and went to investigate. Suddenly, Sonny was shot out of the river, kind of like the Great River was spitting him out (I don't blame it). Sonny arched over the shore and crashed into the grassy ground, yelling in pain. I ran to his side.

Okay, I admit it. I don't completely hate Sonny; he is just annoying sometimes and I have to—*correct* his behavior sometimes. Anyway—

I went to his side, dropping my bow and rolling him onto his back. Sonny clutched his broken arm, his face turning a sickly green. "Moon Song—" he muttered.

"What?" I asked, trying to sit him up, but that made his face worse.

Sonny looked at the surface. "Moon Song. We have—to find her."

"Shh. You are using up too much energy right now. Flame Fall has gone to get her and I'm sure he will find her."

Sonny nodded, rolling over again.

I heard a low moan and saw Astraea panting. "I'll be right back," I told Sonny, rushing to my sister's side and kneeling. "Astraea, are you okay?"

I'll be fine. Is Moon Song—okay? Sonny?

"Sonny is alright, a little sick and hurt, but alright," I answered.

And Moon Song? Astraea's hazel eyes bore into my scalp. *Dakota, where is she?*

"Why do you care so much about her?" I asked sharply.

Astraea's eyes widened in shock, then hardened. *That is none of your concern, Dakota. Where is she?*

I stood, anger surging through me. "She's still in the water. Flame Fall has gone after her." I walked towards the forest.

"Where are you going?" I spun around and saw Oak River starting towards me. I wanted to hate him for beating up Sonny, but I *couldn't*. He was too Oak River-y.

"I'm going to look for a place to sleep. We should rest early tonight and maybe sleep through this rain."

Oak River nodded, his green eyes glowing. "Alright." He walked away.

"You're not the least bit concerned about your sister?" I demanded.

Oak River looked over his shoulder. "Dakota, I have never been in a situation like this before. I feel if I go in after her, I'll only be in the way. If I worry, it'll get everyone else more worked up then they already are. Of course I'm worried, Dakota! Moon Song is the last family I have, and my sister. If she dies I'll be all alone!"

I patted his shoulder. "You have me."

Oak River nodded, but his expression didn't reassure me. I turned and looked at Violet Heart, who was freaking out on the north bank. She ran back a couple meters, tensed her muscles, and ran for the water. Just when I thought she would sprint right into the river, she jumped into the air.

I don't mean 'jumped' like as in a couple of feet; Violet Heart literally soared through the air, clearing the river in a single bound and landed right in front of me. The doe spun around and bleated something to Astraea, who muttered, *In the water*, and passed out. Great.

I turned back to the forest and walked into it, instantly noticing the difference in precipitation. I looked for any mossy clearings like where we had slept last night, but I had no such luck. I did find a great twisted oak that had thick, somewhat horizontal branches that would be exceptional for a sleeping place. The leaves were still heavy at the top, providing a nice big canopy.

I began to make my way back towards the shore and saw Oak River and Violet Heart coming towards me. Astraea was on Violet Heart's back. How that small deer managed to carry a huge, furry, wet wolf, I have no idea. I pointed to the oak and they seemed to get the idea.

"Where are the rest?" I asked Oak River. He pointed back towards the river and I saw Moon Song and Flame Fall, both dripping, and carrying an unconscious Sonny in between them. Flame Fall also had his swords in his hands, which I offered to carry for him. He handed them to me, and they were surprisingly heavy in my hands.

When I got to the oak, Violet Heart had somehow gotten onto one of the higher branches and was monitoring the situation below, Astraea's limp body beside her. Flame Fall and Moon Song were trying to figure out how to get Sonny into the bough. Oak River sat in a branch twisted to look like a chair and was watching the struggle, smiling. Jerk.

Handsome jerk. Minus 'jerk'. Handsome.

Flame Fall climbed into the bough, letting Moon Song hold and try to sustain Sonny's small body. Flame Fall turned around once he had gotten into the bough and lent out his hands. Moon Song attempted to give Flame Fall Sonny, but instead of grabbing his forearms, Flame Fall's grip slipped and grasped his hands instead, resulting in Sonny knocking his head against the trunk. Moon Song winced, trying to push Sonny in front of her. Flame Fall grunted and heaved Sonny upwards.

This time, Flame Fall used too much strength and Sonny flew out of the other side of the bough. Flame Fall gasped and grabbed Sonny's ankles before he could fall to the ground.

I winced as I heard the *thunk* of Sonny's head on the wood. *Again.*

Finally, Flame Fall managed to get Sonny nestled—safely—in the bough, and made himself comfortable on a wide branch. I helped Moon Song into the tree and got settled near Astraea and Violet Heart. With difficulty, I gave Flame Fall his swords back, trying not to drop them onto the forest floor.

At last, I was comfortable and curled up on the wood. Violet Heart made her way to Oak River and curled up, resting her head on his chest. He smiled and petted her head, leaning back and closing his eyes. I shut my eyes, and immediately was spirited off to the dream world.

I woke at the edge of a sunny clearing, the sun glinting on nearby rapids. A small stream wove through the clearing, bending around in an intricate pattern. Something told me this wasn't *my* dream.

Standing in the center of the clearing was Oak River, and he seemed to be waiting for someone. A herd of deer broke through the trees and bounded across the grass a couple meters in front of Oak River. A small doe pulled away from the rest and walked towards Oak River. As she did, the doe glowed and began morphing into a girl. When she reached Oak River, she had long, brown curls flowing over her shoulders, deep blue eyes, a lovely, white dress, and a beautiful, kindly smile.

It was Violet Heart. This was Oak River's dream.

Oak River smiled widely and wrapped his arms around Violet Heart's waist, kissing her on the cheek. Violet Heart giggled and put her arms around his neck. Then the worst thing ever happened.

They kissed.

This was *terrible*. I know that might sound selfish, but Oak River and I had shared *something* this morning, right? Why was *this* happening?!

I could only watch as they kept kissing and laughing. Finally they pulled away from each other, and relief washed over me.

Then Oak River smiled and began tickling Violet Heart's sides. She laughed and darted towards the trees, splashing through the stream on her way. Oak River grabbed the hem of her dress and pulled her back towards him. Violet Heart squealed as she lost her balance and tumbled into the stream, pulling Oak River down with her. They wrestled in the water playfully, splashing each other's faces. Violet Heart climbed out of the river, making a break for the trees, but Oak River was faster.

He jumped at her and they tumbled through the grass until they were a few feet from where I was. I ducked behind a bush, watching through the spindly branches. Oak River had pinned Violet Heart down and was tickling her nonstop.

She giggled and tried to worm out from under him, playfully punching his stomach. Oak River stopped tickling her and grabbed her wrists, pulling her into another kiss. I stared, wide-eyed, at the couple.

Suddenly, the bush disappeared, making me tumble to the ground. I got up and gazed at them, slightly enjoying the look of pure shock on Oak River and Violet Heart's faces.

"Dakota?" Oak River marvelled.

Before I could reply, the ground beneath my feet turned to liquid and I fell through the grass into darkness.

I crashed into a solid stone floor and looked up, seeing a large winged creature. A demon.

He cackled menacingly and looked down at me. "Little mortals. Always being so brave."

He reached down and grabbed the collar of my shirt, lifting me off of my feet.

"No," I said. "This is all a dream! You're not real!"

The demon smiled evilly. "Oh, sweet Dakota. I *am* real, and you are partially right. This isn't a dream. It's a nightmare."

I wanted to scream and sob, but that would be weakness, and part of me knew that even though this was a dream, this demon could do bad things. I looked down and saw that he had a black stone hanging around his neck with a bird engraved in the center of it.

"Black Raven." I clawed his hand, trying to pry it from my neck. "Let me go." My air was getting cut off.

Black Raven grinned and dropped me to the floor, unsheathing a knife and twirling it in his fingers. "Dakota, if I were you, I'd warn your little friends. We will come for you."

"Why do you need us?" I asked, backing away from him.

Black Raven glared at me. "You guys are—*different* from your family members. That is all I will say about it. Do me a favor, will you?"

"What?"

"Accept my present."

"Your present? What—?" My question was cut off by a shriek of pain as Black Raven sliced his knife tip across my cheek.

"Something to remember me by," he snarled. He nodded to someone behind me. "Chain her up."

"This is a dream! You cannot keep me here!" I screamed as someone grabbed my wrists and chained them behind my back. They picked me up and began carrying me away into darkness. I swung my legs wildly as light faded around me. "Let me go! Please! Let me go!"

Black Raven's voice resonated around the cavern: "You cannot hide. You will bend to my will, Da-Kota!"

My eyes flew open. Moon Song was shaking my arm. "Dakota! Wake up!"

I sat up groggily, instinctively reaching for my bow. "What's going on?"

Moon Song's silver eyes shined with concern. "Dakota, you were screaming and crying in your sleep." Moon Song observed my face. "And you're bleeding!"

I ran my finger over my cheek, feeling the warm blood running down my cheek. Black Raven hadn't been messing around. "Must've caught it on the branch while I was sleeping," I told Moon Song.

She looked unconvinced, but nodded and climbed back down to the ground where Astraea, Flame Fall, and a tired Sonny sat around a small fire cooking eggs. *Where had those come from?* Oak River and Violet Heart were still curled up with each other, which made me want to cry again. *It was just a dream. It wasn't real!*

I dropped to the grass, which crunched under my foot. I looked at the sky and saw snow falling. *Winter already?*

Astraea barked softly at me, beckoning me to join her

next to the fire. *Come warm yourself, sister.*

I walked over to her and plopped down on the frosty grass; the large canopy of oak leaves had protected the grass near its trunk from the snow.

A blanket wrapped itself around my shoulders, scaring the heck out of me. "Wha—?"

Flame Fall shrugged. "Don't ask."

I shut my mouth and warmed my hands by the flames. It felt *nice.*

Violet Heart nosed her way into my lap, pulling my blanket around her. She bleated indignantly and began eating mouthfuls of the crunchy grass. She looked in pain as she swallowed her meal. Sonny, who sat next to me, held out a plump red apple and laughed when Violet Heart took it in her mouth and chewed happily.

Flame Fall handed me a piece of toast with a cooked fish on it, which I scarfed down.

Oak River sat down beside me. He seemed to have slept well. His hair was tousled, his green eyes had a warm sparkle in them, and he had a big grin on his face. "Hey guys! How'd you all sleep?"

"Fine," Flame Fall and Moon Song answered.

Sonny took a bite out of his sandwich. "Pretty good considering I was unconscious the majority of the night."

Everyone laughed. Astraea stretched her back. *I slept well. My head feels a lot better.*

Me, Moon Song, and Flame Fall nodded; the rest looked confused.

Violet Heart bleated happily through a bite of apple. Sonny looked at me. "What about you, Dakota?"

"It was good, I guess," I replied, looking at Oak River. His eyes gave me a warning glare: *Not now.*

I could feel Astraea's gaze on me.

Violet Heart's ear went down slightly, which was a sign

of guilt in deer behavior. It actually happened; they met in a dream. *No no no!*

Violet Heart climbed out of my lap and sat beside Oak River, purring (if deer could purr) and finished off her apple.

Astraea stood. *We should get going.*

I stood, going to stand beside my sister. Flame Fall strapped his swords to his back. Moon Song slung a leather satchel over her shoulder and sheathed her boot knives (which I have to admit, was kind of cool). Oak River ruffled his hair back in place, and clipped his sword around his waist.

"Let's get going," Flame Fall said and we marched into the snow.

Chapter 12

Sonny

Something was going on with Dakota and Oak River and Vie. I have a feeling it might have something to do with jealousy; but then again—Nah! Violet Heart is no longer human, That wouldn't make sense.

Before we left, Moon Song suggested putting out the fire, which everyone agreed we should do. Violet Heart's eyes lit up with excitement as she leapt into the flames, rolling around in the embers. I gasped and was going to pull her out, but she didn't seem to have been burned. Actually, it looked like she was *extinguishing* the fire. Magical sisters are so cool.

My jaw dropped in amazement as Vie got to her hooves and licked her fur for a second, then we left the cover of the great oak.

Instantly, the temperature dropped, but I didn't mind. I loved *snow*.

"Winter!" I shouted and leapt into a snowbank, giggling as I made a Sonny-shaped imprint in the four-foot-deep flakes. I jumped to my feet, making many Sonny-shaped imprints into the snow. I felt five again; playing in front of our house while Mother and Father watched from the porch. Violet Heart would always play with me and we would throw snowballs at Flame Fall, which would anger him and result in hard-core snow wrestling.

I grabbed a chunk of snow and formed it into a ball, turning back to the group, which was already ahead of me. I analyzed the scenario: Astraea and Dakota were up front talking, so they wouldn't get in the way; Moon Song was walking with Oak River, probably scolding him; and Flame Fall brought up the rear, watching Vie weave in between our group members. Perfect.

I cocked my arm—my good arm, mind you—and chucked the snowball at Flame Fall from behind. It hit him square in the back of the head, and I watched with satisfaction as snow fell down his collar. Grinning wildly, I sprinted for the group, trying to make it back to Moon Song before Flame Fall realized what I did.

My plan semi-failed.

I was a foot or so from Oak River when I heard something *whoosh* through the air. I ducked and the snowball hit Oak River in the back, making me laugh. Oak River turned, thinking it was me. He smirked and at first I thought I was going to get beaten again; Moon Song apparently felt the same way, because she stopped and rested a hand on her brother's shoulder.

Oak River scooped a ball of snow from the ground and wadded it into a sphere. "Five seconds."

My eyes widened and I ran for the front of the group. Fact: Oak River has terrible aim. The snowball whisked past my shoulder and crashed into Dakota's back, soaking her bowstring and part of her jacket thingy. Dakota spun around, that 'oh-no-you-didn't' look in her teal eyes. She smiled mischievously and hurled a snowball right into Oak River's face.

That girl can *throw*.

The snowball hit Oak River with such force it sent him toppling into the snowy ground.

"Ha!" I laughed aloud, instantly covering my mouth. "Oops."

Then a snowball fight broke out. Even Astraea joined in, flicking paws full of snow into people's faces. Dakota began hurling snow at Oak River nonstop (it was *not* out of friendly fun. She was *mad*. Something was definitely wrong). Violet Heart butted Flame Fall into the snow, bleating playfully. I watched, smiling uncontrollably, when a snowball hit my back, sending a shiver up my spine. I turned to see who the criminal was (yes, it is a crime to assault me), and another ball of snow smacked me in the face, blocking my vision. I wiped my face clear and saw Moon Song readying more ammunition. I chuckled and ran at her, and we engaged in a game of tag. Finally, I barrelled Moon Song into a snowbank, pinning her down. We had a little privacy; the snow came up to my shoulders, and no one could see Moon Song because she had fallen over so, yeah.

Moon Song tried to throw a snowball at me, but I grabbed it from her hand and crushed it in my hand. "Snowballs don't really work for close up combat," I told her, sprinkling the remnants over her face.

"I know," Moon Song replied, her silver eyes glistening. "That's why I have multiple resources." With her free hand, she tickled my sides and I collapsed into a laughing fit beside her. I looked at the sky, noticing that it was the same color as Moon Song's eyes. My hand brushed against Moon Song's, and her fingers wrapped around mine.

"Do you have any idea what happened at the river?" I asked. "I mean me shooting out of the water and stuff."

"Nope." Moon Song sighed. "But we would've been dead if that hadn't happened."

I squeezed her hand. "Yeah. You're so pretty."

Moon Song giggled and kissed me on the cheek. "Thank you, Sun Stream."

I smiled at her, speechless. "I prefer Sonny now."

She raised an eyebrow. "Really? No more 'That doesn't sound manly! Sun Stream sounds better!'"

"Are you imitating me?"

"Yup."

"Well you should work on that; it doesn't even sound like me!" I rolled my eyes.

Moon Song sat up. "The others are starting to leave. We should get going."

I nodded and began to sit up. Moon Song leaned down and kissed me on the lips before standing up, brushing the snow off of her pants, and going to join the group.

I sat there, stunned, before following (it takes a while to get used to your lifelong crush kissing you willingly—not as collateral for jewelry—so don't psych yourself out).

We walked through the woods for a little while, following the oh so trusty nose of 'Madam' Astraea. I am being sarcastic. Those sisters think they own the world sometimes. I'm not actually calling Astraea *madam*. Yuck!

I walked at Moon Song's side, grabbing her hand. "There is something going on between Oak River, Vie, and Dakota," I whispered.

Moon Song glanced at her brother, then my sister, then Dakota. She nodded. "You're right." Moon Song looked at Oak River. "As Oak River being my brother—"

"And Violet Heart being my sister," I put in.

"—We need to find out what this is," Moon Song continued quietly. "Let's call it—" She tilted her head in thought. "Operation OVD."

I nodded in agreement. "Operation OVD it is. I'll find out what I can from Vie. You get what you can from Oak River."

"We can put the pieces together and try to figure out the missing ones that Dakota is hiding," Moon Song said. "Okay."

"Okay," I said, finding myself drowning in the silver pools that one might call her eyes.

"Operation OVD in progress!" Moon Song declared quietly. We giggled in unison, immediately shutting up when Oak River threw us a 'what-are-you-laughing-at?' look, but when he looked away, we started laughing again.

I recommend you stop irritating Oak River if you don't want to break your other arm, Violet Heart told me from where she walked alongside Oak River. Her blue eyes bore into mine, warning me not to protest.

"What did she say?" Moon Song asked me. I remembered that she couldn't hear Vie.

"She told me to stop irritating your brother if I wanted to keep my other arm intact," I translated.

Moon Song smiled, looking at Violet Heart. "Don't worry. Oak River knows what the consequences will be if he messes with Sonny." She squeezed my hand, making me grin uncontrollably.

Violet Heart narrowed her eyes. *Tell your girlfriend to stop talking back to me.*

Moon Song looked at me for the translation. I simply said: "My sister says that was an excellent reply; you didn't get mad or anything. You kept your cool."

Moon Song raised her eyebrows. "Deer is one efficient language."

I nodded, ignoring Vie's look of pure hatred and annoyance. "Yes it is."

"We have some information on Operation OVD," Moon Song commented. "Something romantic may be going on between Vie and Oak River."

I nodded slowly, contemplating the possibilities. "You're right, Silver."

"Silver? Really? Is that a nickname or something?" Moon Song chuckled.

"Yes, Moon Song is too long and elegant for my short-minded tongue."

"What does that mean?" Moon Song asked.

"It takes too much energy to pronounce your name," I concluded.

"Hey, lovebirds," Flame Fall said from behind us. "Get a move on!"

I flushed, embarrassed, and walked faster, Moon Song trailing behind me. "Sonny, it's okay if they know about us, right?"

I nodded. "Yes, it's fine. I just get sensitive about the topic sometimes."

Moon Song kissed me on the cheek. "You're adorable."

I kissed her back, missing her cheek and accidentally kissing her nose instead. Whoops.

Chapter 13

Moon Song

Sonny was so cute when he blushed; his nose turned bright red along with his cheeks. Awesome. Even though he was two years younger than me, he acted like a sixteen year old (*sometimes*). Comments on the nickname?

We walked for what seemed like hours until my feet started aching. It was probably an hour until sunset. I told Sonny I'd be right back and slowly made my way to the front where Astraea and Dakota talked quietly. I decided to not approach them just yet, and listened to Dakota as she spoke.

"It's so frustrating, though! I saw him and her and then him!"

Astraea nodded thoughtfully. *I can see why this would anger you. Oak River kissed you, yes?*

"Yeah! But he kissed her too!"

Calm down, Dakota. We can talk about it after we make camp. It's nothing I'm sure.

Even from just looking at the back of her head, I could tell that Dakota was fuming. "It doesn't seem like nothing! He was *waiting* for her, Astraea. He *knew* she was coming!"

Did it ever occur to you that someone might have told him? Astraea asked, sounding slightly annoyed.

"Well—" Dakota broke off, realizing her sister had a point. "No, I didn't."

Try scanning through all of the possibilities before complaining, Astraea said. *Make yourself useful and look for a good place for camp.*

Dakota scoffed, not liking being bossed around. "Fine."

Moon Song? Astraea didn't even look at me. *Can I help you?*

I stepped up sheepishly. "I was actually going to ask you if we could rest."

We are looking for camp, Astraea explained. She sounded really tired, and it occurred to me that once she came to last night, she probably took the night watch.

"I'll guard tonight," I offered. "You could use some sleep."

Thank you, Astraea said.

"I think I know a place," I said, waiting for Astraea's response. *Take the lead.*

* * *

I took us to a tall waterfall that sprayed freezing water onto us and pooled into a pond seven feet below ground level or so. Dakota stared at me in annoyance.

"Two things: this is a *waterfall*, not a camp. Second, how did you *know* this is here?" she snapped.

"Two answers: my mother travelled through here during her battle days. You know, when she was in a feud with Red Skin, but thank you for that amazing note, Dakota." I turned to the group. "Everyone, this is a waterfall as Dakota mentioned earlier. It is made of water, and falls down a rock, hence the name 'waterfall'."

Oak River and Violet Heart laughed quietly, well, for Vie it would be bleated. The corner of Flame Fall's mouth moved, slowly curving into a smile, while Sonny burst out laughing obnoxiously in the back.

Astraea stepped forward, and I could tell even *she* was trying to keep her cool; the edges of her maw kept twitching into a split-second smile, then she resumed her normal mood. *Not many people can pull off insulting my sister, but you managed it. Congratulations. But Dakota has a point; where is the 'camp' part?*

I opened my mouth. "Ah ha! Thank you for bringing that up, Astraea! I was just getting to that part of the tour. Now, if you will follow me." I walked around the pool and towards the water, seeing an inch-wide ledge behind the freezing sheet of water. Pressing myself to the rock behind the waterfall, I scooted behind the sheet of water. Square behind the waterfall was an opening that led into a cavern.

It was bigger than I thought; the roof went up about fifteen feet or so and about the same depth. The real jaw-dropping feature was the thick fluffy moss that covered the ground and crept up the walls. The whole cavern, I realized, was shaped like a sphere; the roof was domed, the floor curved into the walls, but the floor was flat. The water somewhat protected us from the cold.

Astraea and Dakota came in after me, followed by the others, and satisfaction filled my heart when I saw the incredulous looks on their faces.

Sonny grinned. "This is brilliant, Silver!"

Flame Fall looked at me. "Silver?"

"It's nothing," I answered.

This is pretty good, Astraea commented.

"Sadly," Dakota muttered, raising her voice. "Everyone get settled."

Oak River squinted. "It's pretty dark in here, but okay." He got himself comfortable against a mossy wall, smiling when Violet Heart curled up under his arm. Dakota silently laid on the opposite side of my brother, glaring daggers at him.

Weird.

Flame Fall and Astraea laid down together, resting their heads together. Astraea gave Flame Fall's cheek a little lick and closed her eyes. Cute. I wonder—

Something tingled in the palm of my hand, like a string pulling the skin. I turned my left fist over and opened my fingers. Fingernail-sized balls of light poured from my palm, filling the room with multicolored light. I shut my hand, drawing it to my chest. I noticed everyone's look of pure shock at what I did.

"Sorry about that," I muttered, sitting next to the entrance. Sonny plopped down beside me. "Well that was—interesting."

I smiled and laughed a little. "Yeah."

Sonny nudged me. "Hey, lighten up. Don't go 'Dakota' on me."

Apparently Dakota heard that last part and gave us a nasty glare. I chuckled lightly and whispered, "Speaking of that, I got more information about Operation OVD."

"Oh?" Sonny leaned in towards me. "And what might that be?"

"Dakota said Oak River kissed someone else other than her and it's really bothering her," I whispered. "We need to find out who that was and how Dakota knows this—"

"And how long this has been going on," Sonny suggested.

"Excellent." I shivered and leaned against the wall.

"Cold?" Sonny asked, and grabbed a blanket out of nowhere and wrapped it around my shoulders. "Better?"

"Where did you—?"

"Borrowed it from Dakota," Sonny said with false modesty, making me laugh. I pulled my knives from my boots and twirled them in my hands.

"Get some rest," I told Sonny. "I'm keeping watch tonight, even though I doubt anyone or anything will get in here."

Sonny nodded, his eyes lighting up in different colors due to the lights. "You look like a princess," he said and kissed my nose before settling down beside me. I smooched his forehead as I turned back towards the entrance.

Chapter 14

Dakota

Yes, I was surprised when Moon Song found this perfect place that was comfy and sheltered from the cold, and even more so when she made those cute little light things appear. How did she do that? I have no idea. Okay, now back to my story.

I hated how Oak River and Violet Heart just knew to sleep next to each other. *Hated* it. I'd had a long conversation with Astraea, but she didn't really seem to care. Why would she? A guy would *never* cheat on my sister; back home, all the boys wanted to be with her. Same with how all of the girls wanted to be with Flame Fall. Then Astraea and Flame Fall met and *boom*! Everyone's dreams were crushed except theirs.

I tried turning my attention away from them by closing my eyes, but the dreamworld was not in my favor.

I woke in the clearing again, but this time, Oak River was standing right next to me. "Dakota," he said. "What you saw last night—it wasn't what you think."

"Right," I replied, holding back my anger. "Because you and Violet Heart rolling around in the grass, playing together in the river, and making out means *nothing*."

"Dakota!" He reached for my hand.

"Oak River!" I felt my anger and hatred spilling out. "You were the only thing I had! Mother and Father died, then Astraea! And when we kissed, I thought that meant *something*. Then when Astraea came back, I was ecstatic, but she seemed so distant and when she wasn't, she was talking to Flame Fall. And Violet Heart, I thought she was just going to be there, you know? Like she would be an extra member, but not cause any drama because she's a deer. Well I was wrong! I wake up one night to see you two kissing each other! She's *dead*, Oak River. *Dead!* She might have come back as a deer, but the Violet Heart that I knew is *dead*. The *only* thing keeping me from shooting her down and having her for breakfast is not the fact that everyone here would hate me, but that you in particular have shown somewhat strong affections for her! The worst part about that is that I am showing you mercy. But now I realize I was wrong. I'm no longer keeping her alive for *your* sake; I'm doing it for Astraea. Now I'm wondering if we were *ever* a couple, Oak River, because seeing how easily you dismissed this situation, I don't think you really cared that much that you kissed two girls on the same day. I don't think you *ever* cared!" Tears had welled in my eyes, and as I spilled out my heart to Oak River, so did they.

Oak River stared at me like I had grown a second head, then his expression softened. "Dakota, I'm still here for you. But it's you, not me. You've been really distant lately and—"

"Oh yes," I fumed. "Blame it on me! You still sleep with Violet Heart even though she's a deer! You've shown her more affection than you have *ever* shown me, and I see you more."

"Maybe—"

"Maybe what?" I demanded, balling my fists.

"Maybe we're not ready yet," Oak River finished.

"'*We*'? It's just you, Oak River, who needs to figure out

your loyalty. Not me. Man up." I stormed out of the clearing and felt Oak River's gaze on me. *If he actually wanted me, he would've fought harder.* I risked a glance over my shoulder and saw Oak River walking beside Violet Heart. They were walking towards the stream so closely their bodies were practically touching. *He's already over me.*

I looked forward again right as I fell into a gaping hole of darkness. I hit the ground with a *thud* and saw I was in a massive cavern so tall you couldn't see the roof. Something cold formed around my wrists and I realized they were chains binding me to the wall. I tugged at them, remembering my last dream. *No, this is not real. It's not real.*

A figure emerged from the darkness. Black Raven.

Now that half of his features weren't submerged in shadows like last night, I realized with a jolt of uneasiness that he was kind of attractive. He had tousled black hair, beige eyes, and a handsome chiseled chin. He had light-brown skin that complimented his beautiful eyes. The black stone still hung around his neck, glittering in the light emitted from a nearby torch. He looked about the same age as me.

"It's no use struggling," Black Raven told me. "They won't break."

"Why am I here?" I asked.

Black Raven's eyes brightened. "Excellent topic for discussion." He snapped his fingers and I found myself seated at a dining table filled with fantastic food: a whole roast turkey, ham, deer, fruits, steamed potatoes, a platter of finger sandwiches, biscuits, and a magnificent chocolate cake, my favorite.

Black Raven sat at the other end, munching on an apple. "Help yourself."

I raised an eyebrow. "You're not going to poison me, are you?"

Black Raven shrugged. "I don't know, maybe. No, I'm not."

I narrowed my eyes and grabbed a nearby ham with my hands, digging in. After I finished that off, I snatched an orange and popped the whole thing in my mouth. I seized a strawberry-and-cream sandwich and stuffed it in my mouth, relishing the buttery taste of the pastry.

Black Raven set down his apple. "So to start out, I brought you here because you have the most potential out of anyone."

I swallowed my sandwich, wiping my hands on the table-cloth. "If you think I have potential and you obviously want to use it for your own good, why did you cut my cheek?"

Black Raven's beige eyes sparked. "You're smarter than I thought you'd be."

"And you're more handsome than I thought you'd be, so we're even."

"I thought you and Oak River were—"

"Together? No, he's cheating on me so we are done."

"Oh."

I leaned back in my chair. "Pop quiz: how old are you?"

"A couple hundred years old."

"You age well."

Black Raven looked confused. "Thanks?"

"Do you want to kill me and my friends?"

"Yes—no! Maybe," Black Raven growled. "You're distracting me."

"Really?" I pulled my hair out of its braid and tossed it over my shoulder. "Distracting?"

I could swear Black Raven blushed. "No!" He pounded his fist on the table. "Quiet."

I stopped talking.

"You have a special task."

I twirled a butter knife in my fingers. "Why would I do anything for you?"

"You said yourself that I was attractive, so—"

The butter knife clattered to the floor. "I have no interest in you whatsoever, Black Raven! I feel insulted that you would even think that!" I stood, my face growing hot.

"You're blushing and I need you to tell me where you're going."

I began walking away. "I'm not telling you anything!" As soon as I said that, translucent tendrils of darkness wrapped around my lower body and pulled me back towards Black Raven. I sighed and looked at him, resting my chin in my hands. "Still no."

"Even if I could give you what you wanted?" Black Raven asked.

"You don't know what I want," I spat. "Creep."

"You want Oak River to yourself and not distracted by Violet Heart because it annoys you. Right?" Black Raven's eyes glowed.

"No!"

"No?"

"Knowing you, you're going to accomplish that by killing Violet Heart completely and I don't want that," I said, Astraea's amulet growing warm on my chest. "Why do you need to know anyway?"

Black Raven stared into my eyes. "You're going to the Southern Tribe, yes?"

I slapped Black Raven across the face, making the black tendrils release me and I fell to the ground.

"Dakota!" Black Raven yelled. "Get her!"

I could hear the swooping of wings and something crashed into my back, pinning me to the ground. I tried to roll away but my captor was too strong. "I'll tell everyone about you! I'll tell them your plot and your deception through charm!"

Black Raven laughed somewhere behind me. "No, you won't. I'm going to keep you here—"

"—in a dreamworld? Ha." I knew that he could, reminded by a quick sear of pain on my cheek.

"I gave you that cut and it still bled in reality, yes?" Black Raven asked.

"In reality, am I just going to stay sleeping, or—?"

"Nope, I'm going to actually take you here."

"What do you—" I stopped, feeling something slimy wrap around my feet, snaking its way up my body. I looked down and saw the black tendril. Before I could protest, the cord was around my mouth, then my world went black.

Chapter 15

Sonny

When I woke up, the whole group was in chaos. Flame Fall and Oak River were leaving the cave, their weapons ready. Astraea was pacing the ground, a quiet growl rumbling in her throat. Violet Heart leaned over Moon Song as she pointed to various parts of a map. I didn't see Dakota anywhere, but her bow and arrows were propped against the wall.

I sat up, readying Tiny. I walked over to Moon Song.

"—are going to check by the river," she was saying.

"What's going on?" I asked.

"Dakota disappeared. She wasn't here when we woke, and she left her bow and quiver, which is *not* like Dakota," Moon Song answered grimly. "Astraea is really worried, and Oak River keeps rambling on and on about how this is his fault." She looked at me and I knew we were both thinking the same thing: *Operation OVD.*

Violet Heart looked back and forth between us. *What's going on? Do you*—She stopped, her eyes widening.

"Vie?" I got down on my knees. "What's going on?"

The dream—it can't be.

"Violet Heart, care to explain?" I asked. Moon Song looked extremely confused.

Dakota saw us in a dream and then she fell into a pit of darkness. Then the next night, the same thing happened. Nothing like this has ever happened before, and only one person is capable of such cruelty.

"Stop with the secrets!" I screamed. Astraea turned and looked at me like 'what the—?'

Dakota was taken from one dream and into another, which is rare, and then from that dream, she was taken from reality by a demon. That's not good.

"Oh."

"What is it?" Moon Song asked.

"Long story short, she met this demon dude in a dream and he took her from the real world," I explained.

"Oh." Moon Song rolled up her map and tucked it in her satchel. "Astraea, Dakota's not here," she called to the wolf.

Astraea and Moon Song seemed to have a silent conversation before the wolf nodded and went to the entrance, bounding out after Flame Fall and Oak River.

"She's going to retrieve the boys," Moon Song told me, standing. Violet Heart's ears were pinned back against her head as she laid down on the other side of the cavern, staring at her hooves. A couple minutes passed until Astraea entered the cave with Flame Fall and Oak River. Both boys looked sullen, their weapons hanging at their sides.

Astraea barked something at Moon Song, who nodded and translated, "Astraea says we should leave. It won't do us any good just waiting around for Dakota; her captor won't just give her back because we wait politely."

"That's a good plan," I agreed. Everyone turned to look at me. "I mean, I want Dakota back too; she's my friend. But the demon dude took Dakota for a reason, and it probably wasn't to have her at his place for the night." My eyes widened. "Oh, gods, I didn't mean—"

Flame Fall chuckled lightheartedly, "Come on, let's go."

I nodded, trying to hide my flushed face. Astraea led the group out of the den, Oak River bringing up the rear. Vie trotted nervously at Flame Fall's side, casting quick glances back at Oak River. Once we cleared the waterfall, snow-flakes clung to my eyelashes.

I leaned towards Moon Song, who walked a foot or so ahead of me. "It was nice doing business with you."

Moon Song slackened her pace so she walked at my side. "What does that mean?"

"Operation OVD is complete."

"No. We still need to find out who 'her' is!" Moon Song whispered.

I raised an eyebrow. "Really?"

Moon Song scoffed, "You know who it is?"

I gestured towards Violet Heart, smiling at Moon Song's look of shock. She whispered, "No, that's not possible it—" She broke off, realization creeping across her face. "Oh!"

"Believe me now?" I asked, slipping my hand into hers. Moon Song butted my shoulder with her head and sighed, "Sure, Sonny."

"Awesome." I couldn't help notice the way the snow fell onto her hair, making her even more beautiful (if that was possible). Moon Song's silver-blue pendant glowed with unnatural light.

"Why can't you understand Vie, but you can hear Astraea?" I asked.

Moon Song looked down at her pendant. "It must allow me to hear family, I guess."

"Family? But Astraea is—"

"My cousin," Moon Song said. "My father, Blood River, and her mother, Ocean Lotus, are siblings. Well half-siblings, technically. They have the same mothers but different fathers."

"Oh!" I said. "Wait but that means Oak River and Dakota— oh no."

"Yeah—That's weird," Moon Song admitted. "Should we tell them?"

"Later," Moon Song decided, glancing back at Oak River. "He's already sad about Dakota. It won't help to remind him they're related."

I nodded. "Makes sense." We held hands and walked along the path. It made my insides turn to see Astraea so worked up; she was usually the most composed out of all of us. Astraea told Moon Song that we were about an hour or so away from the Southern Tribe.

* * *

We reached the Southern Tribe's entrance at dusk. It was a huge cave that could easily have fit ten of our little caverns inside of it. We walked inside, our weapons ready. Even Moon Song (who I think is going to become our medic) had her tiny knives ready. Astraea's hackles were raised with tension, and Vie's back was arched.

Suddenly a weighted net shot out of the darkness and within the blink of an eye had pinned Astraea, Violet Heart, and Flame Fall to the ground. Astraea howled in outrage, while Violet Heart bleated angrily.

I shifted sideways, trying to see through the gloom, then I heard a *snap* and dust scattered as a net enclosed around me, Oak River, and Moon Song. The net was pulled into the air by thick ropes. My foot got caught in the net so when the motion had settled, I was hanging upside down inside the net, eye level with Moon Song and a fuming Oak River. "Nice job, mouseling," he muttered. Moon Song didn't seem to have heard, as she was busy trying to cut through the net with her knife (I had dropped Tiny when I valiantly got shot into the air).

Figures crept out of the shadows, bearing spears, daggers,

knives, and other assorted weapons. I don't fancy people holding weapons while looking at me menacingly.

A rather muscular man stepped forward. "What is your business here?"

I was about the speak when Moon Song cupped her hand over my mouth and looked down at the man. "We have come to seek your aid," she said.

The man raised an eyebrow. "And what might you need aid for?"

Moon Song looked at Oak River for help. I pried her hand from my lips. "Who cares? Be a gentleman and let us down from here! Then maybe we'll tell you."

Mr. Buff (which is what I decided would be a good name for him, considering he was about one-and-a-half feet taller than myself—at least!) grunted, signaling to a lithe woman, who threw a tiny knife like a javelin and sliced through the ropes holding us up. I let out a startled squeak as Oak River, Moon Song, and myself fell to the ground.

I untangled my foot from the net and got to my feet. I spotted Tiny a little ways away and went to grab it, but Mr. Buff kicked it away.

How dare he kick the almighty Tiny!

I huffed and went to stand beside Moon Song and Oak River, who both had readied weapons. *Dang.*

The man signaled to his followers and they formed a tight circle around us. Someone threw the net off of Flame Fall, Astraea, and Violet Heart.

Vie stood and shook the dirt from her fur. She looked at me with her soft blue eyes. *This is where I leave. We were your escorts, that's all.* She gracefully bounded through our bewildered Southern Tribe friends and out of the cave, disappearing into the trees.

Just leave us like that, Vie. What a great big sister, I thought. *Coward.*

Mr. Buff smiled. "Looks like your hooved companion chickened out."

Oak River stared disbelievingly at the trees were my sister had vanished. I felt that same way, man.

Mr. Buff nodded to his tribemates, watching with pleasure as they bound my hands behind my back with *really* itchy rope (it was also painful, as I still had a somewhat broken arm). I snarled as Oak River, Moon Song, and Flame Fall received the same treatment. My group was disarmed of their weapons (Mr. Buff personally searched Moon Song, but didn't bother checking inside her boots where her knives were stored. I swear he was only interested in her upper half).

As the Southern Tribe bullies hustled us towards the shadows, Astraea howled and threw herself at a Native standing behind me. Our other captors pointed their weapons at Astraea, ready to attack.

My eyes widened. "No! Don't—" Astraea let out a blood curdling screech (if wolves could screech) and ran out of the cave and into the forest. *Two escorts gone.*

"Come on! Stop dawdling!" Mr. Buff scolded. I turned back towards him, my eyes stretching wide when I saw a pitch black hole that tunneled deep into the rock yawning in front of me. Mr. Buff stood next to it.

"It's a hole," I observed.

The tall ninja girl, who had cut us down from the nets, rolled her eyes (I'm pretty sure she did; it was hard to tell in the dark) as she walked past me. She jumped into the hole, her black hair disappearing against the darkness.

"You expect us to *jump*?" I asked.

Mr. Buff nodded. Another Native leapt down the hole silently. I was shoved from behind and almost fell into the hole of doom.

Flame Fall looked at me and hesitantly slid down the

tunnel. Moon Song sighed, "It's not a trap if their own went down it," and jumped after my brother.

Three more Southern Tribe members disappeared into the hole. Oak River looked at me, waiting for my divine self to follow them into the tunnel.

"I'm not waiting," someone grunted and I felt a sharp push from behind me and I tumbled down the hole. Darkness was abundant in this tunnel; it seemed to go down forever. And ever. And ever—I started to get scared that this led to an underground lava chamber and I would be a Sonny Side up breakfast. That would *not* be good.

The tunnel began to fill with orange light, and I shot out of the underpass onto dirty stone. I grunted, sitting up and examining my surroundings. My mouth fell open.

I had landed in a cavern. But it was *huge*; the roof went up so high it was lost in shadows, and the chamber was big enough to have housed Ashinders. The sides of the cavern were made of stone and dirt, and built inside of them were homes. Doors were embedded in the dirt and windows were carved into the side, behind them rooms full of furniture. A few yards from where I sat was a marketplace, and even from here, I could smell the tasty aromas of the food stands. My stomach growled loudly.

Ninja Girl approached me and pulled me to my feet. "Move or the others will crush you."

I blinked at her. "Yeah, yeah, okay."

We moved just as Oak River slid out of the mouth of the tunnel, which was built into the side about three feet from the ground. Mr. Buff and his friends came after him and started herding me, Moon Song, Oak River, and Flame Fall towards massive double doors at the very end of the cavern.

"What *is* this place?" I asked, looking around at all the people that walked around the grotto.

Ninja Girl sighed. "This is the Southern Tribe."

Chapter 16

Moon Song

When I saw the Southern Tribe I thought, *Wow, they sure know how to impress guests.*

The leader of the group—what did Sonny call him? Mr. Buff? Ha—seemed to like me. A lot. I didn't like him though. He was too full of himself.

I stared at the dirt cave houses in awe as we were herded across the cavern, receiving interested looks from the villagers. Some even stopped to watch us pass. I saw a little girl run over to an older woman and point at us, her braided pigtails bouncing up and down. I almost laughed.

Mr. Buff walked to my side and looked at the massive oak doors, which were decorated with gold swirl designs. "That's where the chief and his family live. That's where we are going."

"Really?" I asked.

Mr. Buff nodded. "Yeah. I'm going to tell you this: Chief and his wife found a baby while they were exploring and decided to adopt her. She is *not* an alien, whatever you might think."

I tilted my head, confused. "Okay?"

"Glad you understand. I'm Hawk Feather, by the way. What's your name?" he asked.

I sighed. "Nice to meet you, Hawk Feather. My name is of no importance to you, so you needn't know it and we are going to keep it that way."

Hawk Feather's eyes widened at my sharp tone. "Don't you—" He stopped as we reached the double doors. Two guards stood at either side. Hawk Feather nodded at one and the guard opened the doors. We walked inside, five other Southern Natives with us.

Inside was yet another cavern, maybe a quarter of the size of the village, but still huge. At the far end was a chair elaborately carved from mahogany wood, engraved with scenes of Natives dancing around fires and the chiefs watching happily. On the back of the chair was the face of a man that looked strangely familiar.

"Chief Wild Grass!" the guard said. "Your son is here with intruders!"

I now noticed a house embedded in the stone behind the throne-ish thing. A muscled man stepped from the door, a crown of feathers on his head. He had deep, brown eyes and a well defined face. He was closely followed by a middle-aged woman, who must have been the Chief's wife. She had the same colored eyes as Hawk Feather and her graying hair was swept over one shoulder.

But behind *her* was the strangest looking girl I'd ever seen.

She looked to be about sixteen, but her skin was *white*. Not completely white, mind you, but relatively white. Her eyes were teal, like Dakota's, but darker and more welcoming. The strangest thing of all was her hair. It was red-orange, and I could tell it wasn't just from the torchlight. It was *definitely* an alien life-form.

Both women had beautiful silk gowns on, and the white girl's hair was braided into an elegant bun. Wow!

The Chief sat on the throne examining us, while his wife and (alien) daughter stood on either side of him. I looked to my right and saw my brother standing at my side. His green gaze was fixed on the white girl and I could tell his jaw was on the verge of dropping open.

Chief Wild Grass gestured to Hawk Feather. "Please explain why you have brought our enemy into my home."

Hawk Feather bowed quickly. "Father—Chief, these Natives were wandering around the entrance with weapons and demonized animals."

I lifted my chin. "Sir, if I may speak."

Chief Wild Grass looked at me and then at Hawk Feather, then at me again. He gestured for me to go on.

"Those animals were not demonized. They were merely reincarnations of tribemates that have passed. One was their sister." I looked back at Flame Fall and Sonny. "And the other was—a friend." I was going to say Dakota's sister, but I had almost forgotten that she wasn't here. "They were our escorts from our home to here. But they are gone now; they left once we arrived at the cave—"

"They attacked our guard!" a Native protested, and I realized it was the girl with the ninja knives. "Sir, they—"

"Hush, Dawn Whisper. Let the girl finish talking," Chief Wild Grass interrupted.

I nodded my thanks. "They only attacked because your guard was right on the verge of impaling us with his weapons. Anyway, we have come to seek your aid."

Wild Grass nodded thoughtfully, and the white girl leaned over and whispered something in his ear. In the torchlight, she looked like a goddess. Wild Grass nodded and stood.

"Hawk Feather," he began. "Take those two to the dungeons." He pointed to me. "I want her—" He pointed to someone behind me; I didn't turn to see who. "—and him."

Hawk Feather exclaimed disbelievingly, "Why him?"

"He seems like the type of person who would slip away easily," Wild Grass explained. "Those two in my house now!"

The Ninja Girl, Dawn Whisper, grabbed one of my bound arms and marched me towards the Chief's home. I heard grunting behind me and tried to turn to see who it was, but the Chief was blocking my view. Dawn Whisper walked inside the house and closed the door behind us, throwing me onto a wool rug. I sat upright, trying to break my bonds.

"It's no use," Dawn Whisper sighed with sarcastic sadness, "I've been working on knots since I was ten; I'm the best in the tribe."

"That's lovely, but I'm not trying to untie the ropes," I said as I tucked my knees under me. I slowly pulled down the top of my boot, searching for my knife. Then I felt it—the leathery texture of the hilt. I carefully pulled it out of the boot as to not attract any of Dawn Whisper's attention. Precariously, I sawed the edge of the blade against the rope, satisfaction rippling through me as I heard the quiet *snap* of the ropes.

Wild Grass marched into the room, followed by the white girl, his wife, another guard, and Sonny. The guard tossed Sonny down beside me and went to sit by Dawn Whisper.

Wild Grass sat on a chair across from us. "So, what do you need aid for?"

I glanced over and saw anger boiling in Sonny's eyes. Sonny burst out, "You mean you didn't see any of the smoke, fire, or ashes pluming from our village? *Are you serious?*"

Wild Grass' eyes widened and Dawn Whisper and the other guard bared their weapons.

Sonny continued, "Our village got burned to the ground, and as far as we're concerned, we are the only survivors! Our families and friends are dead, and it's not fair that they die and we live, because it tortures the living daylight out of us, and I don't know about the rest of my group, but I can't stand knowing that my parents and sister are dead, and that there was something I could have and should have done about it! I saw my father die! Do you know how that feels? And then my hopes soared higher than the clouds when I found out Violet Heart had come back reincarnated, but then she leaves us as soon as we get here! The only family I have left is Flame Fall, and he is probably chained up in your dungeons right now!" Tears trailed paths in the dirt on Sonny's face. He shook violently, and at the same time, my bonds snapped loose.

I tucked my knife back into my boot; fortunately, no one had noticed my blade. I was going to make a run for it, but Sonny needed me.

I wrapped an arm around Sonny's shoulders and put my other hand on his. Sonny didn't look at me and kept crying. I glanced at our listeners: Wild Grass and his wife were wide-eyed, the white girl was staring at the floor, probably unsure what to do, and the guards had noticed my hands were loose and were starting to get impatient.

"Sonny," I whispered softly, "Hey, look at me." I lifted my hand from his hands and turned his face so he was looking at me. I wiped the tears from his cheeks. "It's going to be fine. We'll see Vie again."

Sonny nodded and sniffled, shaking tears from his face. He looked at our audience. "Sorry. It's been an emotional past couple of days."

Dawn Whisper started towards me. "Chief, her bonds—"

"Hush." Wild Grass stood. "Thank you for talking with us." He paused. "Would you mind telling me your names?"

I looked self-consciously at Dawn Whisper. "Uh—"

"Silver and Sun Stream," Sonny replied. I smiled at him.

Wild Grass nodded to his guards. "Thanks for your time."

"No, thank you," I replied. "And sir—"

"Dawn Whisper, Lion Claw, take these two to the dungeons," Wild Grass said.

Chapter 17

Dakota

After the smoke tendrils nearly suffocated me, I woke up in a well-lit chamber. One side was barred, so I guess that would make the room I was in a prison of sorts. I sat up and looked around.

Footsteps sounded from outside my jail. I spun around, surprised to see Black Raven watching me. I stumbled to my feet, which sent spots dancing across my vision. Once my eyesight cleared, I stormed to the bars, grabbing Black Raven's (gorgeous) hair and pulling him towards me. "Where am I? Why haven't I woken up?" I demanded.

Black Raven sighed. "Let go of me and I'll tell you."

I rolled my eyes and let go of his hair. "I'm waiting."

"Thank you," he said, rubbing his head. "First off, you are in my VIP: Very Important Prison. Second, you have woken up; you're really here."

My eyes widened. "What?"

"Are you wondering about the VIP or the waking up?" Black Raven asked, his beige eyes sparkling mischievously.

"Both."

Black Raven nodded and walked straight through my prison bars, so he was standing right next to me. "Sit, please."

He gestured behind me and I saw two poofy chairs facing each other.

"What—" I began.

Black Raven held up his hand. "Don't ask."

I shut my mouth and sat down. Black Raven sat across from me. "So, let's start out with the VIP. The Very Important Prison is for very important prisoners. You, Dakota, are a very important prisoner. It will take care of whatever needs you have that are within reason, so say if—"

"—If I'm craving a bowl of soup," I suggested, and immediately a bowl of Mother's homemade soup appeared in my hands.

Black Raven nodded. "Exactly. The room also changes with your will, so if—"

"—If I wanted to be back where I was before you brought me here," I interrupted, and immediately the room morphed to the size and shape of the small circular cavern, but it seemed empty without everyone here or Moon Song's floating lights (*don't* tell her I was impressed because I wasn't; I was just feeling high admiration and respect towards her, that's all).

"Why am I here?" I asked, looking down at my bowl. "I want to go home."

"You have no home, Dakota. Last I checked, it was a pile of ashes," Black Raven said as he flicked a speck of dirt from his shoulder.

My bowl fell out of my hands as I shot to my feet. "I *do* have a home! It's with my friends and family: Flame Fall, Oak River, Astraea, Sonny, and even Moon Song, I guess. They are my home, and even if Astraea isn't really here, she's the only family left, I—"

"I'm going to stop you right there," Black Raven sighed. "Astraea's not your only living family."

I tilted my head. "My grandfather Red Wolf is dead along with his wife. And Grandfather Red Skin is dead—"

"You're overcomplicating things." Black Raven ran his fingers through his hair (he looked *so* cute when he did that). "They were with you before I brought you here."

I narrowed my eyes in thought. "This is a trick. Astraea is the only living family I have left that I am aware of—"

"Oak River."

I squinted in confusion. "Pardon?"

"Oak River."

"What about him? He's not related to me in any way."

"Your mother, Ocean Lotus, and his father, Blood River, are siblings, yes? Well, half-siblings, technically, but still—" Black Raven let me mentally figure this out.

"Oh, Eagle Spirit. He's my *cousin*?" I asked disbelievingly.

Black Raven nodded.

"Oh, gods, no. I kissed him! Multiple times! We made out! Oh, gods, does he know?" I paced the small cavern, which stretched out into the normal stone cave again.

Black Raven shook his head. "Not yet."

I sighed, "Let's keep it that way, please." I stared at the wall in front of me, my back facing Black Raven, as I ran the scene of me and Oak River (my cousin! Ugh!) through my head.

"Okay."

"Thanks, Black Raven, I really—" I spun around, nearly toppling over when I found Back Raven's face six inches from mine. "—appreciate it."

"No problem," Black Raven said. "You want to know why you're here?"

"Yes."

"My boss wants your heads, and you're the bait, Dakota, but—"

I gasped and pushed past him. "'Bait?' What is that supposed to mean? You can't keep me here forever! You'll drop me off somewhere in the valley and I'll find my way back to my friends. They know it's a trap; Astraea knows a ton since she's been dead."

"Astraea is no longer with your friends." Black Raven sat back down on his chair. "She left once they reached the Southern Tribe, along with your little deer friend."

"They were only our escorts, that's all," I said, trying to convince myself that Astraea wouldn't abandon us. "They had elsewhere to be."

Black Raven chuckled and walked back towards the bars. "Tell yourself what you need to, Dakota." He stepped through the iron bars. "Enjoy your stay here." Then he disappeared in a cloud of black smoke.

I huffed in frustration. Turning back to the cave, I closed my eyes, wishing I was back home. The air around my head churned, causing my hair to blow into my face. I opened my eyes and gasped. I was standing in the living room of my house. The fire crackled, waves of warmth flooding the house. It all looked the same: the well-dusted furniture, the cute little kitchen, and the sparkling-clean windows. At first I couldn't believe it; but then I remembered the cave could change into any place. I had wished to get home, and it took me there.

Even though I wasn't actually *home*, I smiled and ran to my room. Both beds were clean and made, and the room looked really really nice. I jumped onto my bed, laughing when my face hit my pillow. It smelled of home.

I sat up and decided to experiment. Shutting my eyes, I willed my house to transform to my liking, and when I opened my eyes, I was sitting on a king-sized bed. Me and my sister's room had transformed into a beautiful room that was fit for royalty; the neat bed, two beautiful mahogany dressers, and a little living space at the far end of the room. I smiled and laughed loudly, flopping down on the bed again.

For a couple minutes, I just laid there, speechless. Then I jumped up and ran to my parents' room, which had transformed into a gorgeous bathroom, complete with a bathtub.

I turned on the bath water and tied my hair up in a bun. I stripped off my clothes, the cool air sending shivers up my back. I stepped up to the bath, testing the water with my fingers. It was nice and warm, and I couldn't wait to get in.

My bare legs and arms were bruised and scarred from our journey. When we had crossed the Great River, a branch that was submerged three feet underwater had been driven into my leg. Lucky for me, the wood hadn't pierced my skin, but from my ankle up to my knee on my right leg, a wide, pink scar stretched through my brown skin.

I grimaced at the wound and climbed into the warm water, sighing as my muscles relaxed. Maybe this prison wouldn't be as bad as I thought.

Chapter 18

Sonny

I was definitely getting taller. When we started this journey, I was eye-level with Moon Song's nose. Maybe a little less. Yes it's embarrassing, and yes, I now regret sharing it with you. But now, I could easily look over the top of Silver's head. Flame Fall said puberty is the worst thing ever. I don't know what's going on with him, but I *love* it!

Anyway—

The Ninja Girl—Dawn Whisper—and Lion Claw escorted us to the dungeons, which were a lot nicer than I expected dungeons that were a hundred feet underground to be. Fortunately, the cells were clean and cobweb-free. Unfortunately, everyone got their own cell. Fortunately (again), the cells were bunched together in groups of four, and my friends were alone in their own little group. Dawn Whisper tossed me into a cell that neighbored Oak River, muttered, "Demon spies," and locked my cell door with three different locks (she must have telepathy or something because somehow she knew I was a 'slippery little mouseling' as Dakota would say).

Dawn Whisper glared at me for a moment and walked up the winding stairwell that eventually led to the entrance of the prison. Lion Claw tossed Moon Song in my other neighboring cell, put one lock on her door, and walked after his tribemate.

I turned to Moon Song. "*One* lock?"

Moon Song tilted her head in confusion, looked at my cell door, then broke into a fit of laughter. "She must know you're a trickster!"

Flame Fall was passed out cold, his dark hair blending in with the dirt covered stone. Oak River had his back to me and was staring at the entrance, as if waiting for someone. I settled down and looked around the dungeon.

The prison itself wasn't terrifying; it was the fact that the dungeon was so *empty* that told me the Southern Tribe either didn't make a lot of enemies, scared them all off, or got rid of them quickly. I wasn't enthusiastic about the latter possibility.

The cell was well-lit with torches that emitted warm orange-yellow light. It was about ten feet tall and fifty feet in length and width. The cell groups were placed into three neat columns. We were near the end of the second column, which told me that these folks didn't exactly trust us. I don't blame them.

I looked at Moon Song, then at Oak River, then back at Moon Song. Finally, I turned to Oak River. "Hey Oak River?"

Oak River jumped a foot in the air. Again, I don't blame him; it was pretty quiet in the dungeon. He turned to look at me. "What?"

"I have two questions: one, who are you waiting for? Two, what do you think happened to Dakota?" I whispered.

Oak River narrowed his eyes. "One, nobody. I'm just looking at the entrance—"

"Intently," I put in.

"—Two, I don't know, but I hope that Black Raven guy doesn't hurt her, or else I'll be p—"

I held up my hand. "I get it. You'll be angry." I turned

around and slumped against the bars. An idea sparked in my head. I turned back to Oak River and whispered, "Do you like that white girl?"

That made Oak River *blush*; his cheeks went red in a record time of one-half second! Whoa! Kidding, I wasn't actually timing him, but his cheeks flushed like no one's business.

"That's none of your concern," he spat.

"Okay, if you say so," I shrugged. "Dakota might get upset if she finds you're cheating on her."

Oak River huffed. "Sonny—"

"Sonny," Moon Song cut in. "Stop."

I turned and stared at my girlfriend (Ha. I love being able to say that I have a girlfriend, and that it's Moon Song).

"I have an escape plan," Moon Song said. "Oak River, wake up Flame Fall. He's closer to you."

Oak River obeyed and shook my brother awake. Flame Fall sat up groggily, his dark, brown hair sticking out on one side and flat on the other. Typical bed-head.

Everyone gathered around each other as close as they could and Moon Song explained, "When we came in here, I saw a sort of stable. It had horses, and beyond that there was another set of double doors that opened into another exit, I think. The ground of the floor behind the doors gently sloped upwards, and light faintly came through."

"And you saw all this from a distance?" Flame Fall sounded impressed.

Moon Song blushed and nodded. "I think if we can somehow escape from here, we would be able to steal the horses and get above ground."

"How about we knock out all the guards here and fight all the rest?" Oak River suggested.

I sighed. "Because these worms have more experience fighting underground than we do, because it's an entire village more than double the size of Ashinders, and because it's well guarded, that's not going to work," I said. "But I know what will! I think if we can get above ground, *then* we can start fighting and battling and stuff, okay?"

"Great thinking, Sonny," Moon Song said.

"Okay," Flame Fall, Oak River, and I said in unison.

"One question," I said. "How did you escape your bonds?"

Moon Song smiled and put her hand into her boot, unsheathing a tiny bit of one of her knives. That girl has *skills*. She sheathed them quickly as footsteps echoed from the staircase.

Dawn Whisper and Hawk Feather made their way towards us, their faces grim. Behind them, Lion Claw dragged a screaming girl, who was about the age of twelve, and tossed her into a cell across from me. Her black hair was cropped along her jawline and longer in the front so that it swept in front of her eyes, which were piercing amber.

"Little rat!" Lion Claw taunted as he locked up the girl, marching back up the staircase. The girl panted heavily and wiped the sweat from her forehead with her grimy sleeve.

Hawk Feather stopped at my cell and looked at Moon Song. "And what might you be discussing here?"

Moon Song sighed in exasperation. "Nothing, Hawk Feather. Just talking of how much we miss our destroyed home, our lost family." She was laying it on *thick*.

Hawk Feather faked an *okay-I-would-help-but-I-don't-want-to smile*. "We are trying to decide what to do, Moon Song,"

Moon Song laughed without humor. "Yeah, your father made that quite clear."

Hawk Feather suddenly became interested in his footwear.

Moon Song gestured with her index finger for Hawk Feather to come closer. "I need to tell you something."

Hawk Feather raised his eyebrow suspiciously, and I huffed

with disapproval as Mr. Buff unlocked Moon Song's cell and sat beside her. "What is it?"

Moon Song leaned closer to him, and that's where I lost it. I shot to my feet, but then Moon Song gave me that *don't-do-it look* and I sat back down, fuming.

Moon Song unsheathed her knives and clubbed the top of the hilts into Hawk Feather's temples. Hawk Feather crumbled unconscious to the ground, the cell keys clattering out of his hands. Dawn Whisper shouted in protest and started towards Moon Song. As Dawn Whisper entered Moon Song's cell, her sword bared, I grabbed her long black hair and yanked the locks towards me. Dawn Whisper screamed in agony as her head pulled into the metal bars. She fell to the ground beside Hawk Feather.

Moon Song grabbed the keys from the ground. "Let's get out of here."

Chapter 19

Moon Song

Sonny was definitely getting taller. When we started this journey, he was at least two inches shorter than me. Now he was two inches *taller* than me.

I unlocked Flame Fall's cell first, then Oak River's. Finally, I unlocked Sonny's very many locks.

Clink. Clink. Clink.

Sonny clambered out of his cell and hugged me tightly. I pushed him away and relocked my cell, imprisoning our guards for a while. I gathered everyone around me and grabbed Sonny's hand. "Let's go!"

Oak River and Flame Fall ran for the entrance, but Sonny hesitated at the cell of the little girl Lion Claw had locked up earlier. Her amber eyes were sharp with dread, and along her cheek was a red scab that looked strangely like a dagger mark.

She stared at me, her expression a mix of warning and fear. "I didn't do anything wrong. I only stole some food."

Sonny grabbed the keys from my hand and unlocked the girl's cell, offering his hand to her. "You can come with us."

The girl hesitated before grabbing Sonny's hand. Sonny gestured for me to follow him as he ran after Oak River and Flame Fall. I ran after him and noticed the girl was lagging behind a little.

"Let me lead the way!" the girl shouted, gaining speed and pushing past my brother. "I know this place better than the rest of you."

Oak River looked back at me and shrugged, running after the girl. Finally we emerged into the main part of the village. No one seemed to have noticed our escape yet, which was good.

"Follow me," the amber-eyed girl said. She pressed herself against the wall closest to us and almost immediately disappeared in the shadows. Whoa.

Sonny pushed past Oak River and Flame Fall and slipped into the shadows.

I muttered, "Eagle Spirit, I don't like her," and followed my boyfriend (Ha. I love being able to say I have a boyfriend). I heard Flame Fall and my brother quietly follow me, hardly making a sound. As we slipped around the perimeter of the cavern, nearing the stables, I heard shouting behind us.

Oh no. Hawk Feather and Dawn Whisper were awake. I tapped Sonny on the shoulder. "Tell her to hurry up."

Sonny looked behind me and nodded, turning to the girl. "Can you hurry up, please?"

The girl nodded and crouched down. "Do you want your weapons back?"

"Yeah, that would be nice," Oak River answered.

"Okay, you," she pointed to Sonny, "come with me. The rest of you, get the horses ready for departure. I suggest you," she pointed to Oak River, "make sure that the guards don't reach the other two while they get the horses ready."

Oak River nodded, obviously shocked at the girl's orders.

The girl stood. "Let's go." She grabbed Sonny's wrist and ran into a passing crowd of people.

I sighed in exasperation and ran for the stables. Inside were more people than I expected; a dozen at least. Half of them were heavily armed, and started towards us when we entered the stables.

Flame Fall and Oak River bared their fists. Behind them, the big double doors swung closed, shutting us in. *Of course.*

I unsheathed my knives and started towards the nearest guard, kicking him in the gut and whaling the side of his head with my knife hilts. He crumpled to the ground, his sword clattering to the ground.

The other half that weren't guards were villagers tending to the horses. I approached them, my knives bared. "Get out of here. *Now!*" I growled.

The villagers nodded and obediently ran out of the stables, two guards following them out. Oak River and Flame Fall had knocked out the rest of the guards, and someone was banging on the door.

"It's guards," Oak River said.

"IT'S NOT GUARDS!" Sonny shrieked from the other side of the door. "LET US IN!"

Flame Fall pushed the doors open a tiny bit, enough for Sonny and the girl to slip in and for me to catch a glimpse of dozens of guards rushing towards us.

Sonny distributed the boys' weapons while I untied the horses from their pens. "Hurry up!"

Flame Fall climbed onto a black horse, Oak River mounted a brown horse, while Sonny (clumsily) got on a white horse.

My eyes fell on a well-groomed, muscular, silver horse. I rushed to its side, swinging onto its back using the lead attached to its muzzle.

The girl grabbed one of the unconscious guard's crossbows and climbed on behind Sonny.

I really don't like that girl.

Sonny took up the lead in his hands, and using it like reins, spurred the horse into motion. I followed, Flame Fall behind me, and Oak River bringing up the rear. We galloped up to the entrance as the double doors burst open and two dozen men opened fire on us with razor-sharp arrows. "Street rat!" they yelled at the girl.

I pressed myself against the back of my gelding, trying to avoid getting pierced. Then the girl turned around and fired at the guards with her crossbow. She shot five men and stunned two, and three went running for help. That left two very angry men that were trying to kill us. We then turned a corner and I lost sight of them, though I could still hear their insults: "Street rat!" and "Thieving pest!"

I focused on what was ahead in front of us. Light was beginning to fill the tunnel, giving me more and more hope that we would reach the woods.

I smiled and urged my steed to go faster, and soon I was leading the group, and finally we broke out of the tunnel. Fresh, cold air washed down my throat, making me want to scream with joy, "HA HA! I'M INVINCIBLE!" but that wouldn't exactly count towards our not dying.

I sped into the trees, slowing my horse down to a walk. Oak River, Flame Fall, Sonny, and the girl caught up to me, panting. The girl's amber eyes stood out against the white of the snowy forest as she scanned the horizon for any Southern Tribers.

"They're not going to catch us for a while," I told her.

"You don't know that. No one can be sure," she muttered as she turned to leave.

"Hold on." I looked at my peers. "Can we stop for a moment?"

Our group pulled over and rested in a thick grove of birch trees. I dismounted my horse and tied the lead to a tree. Unsheathing my knives, and twirling them in my hands. I looked at the girl. "I have some questions."

"Ask away," the girl said as she dusted off her dirt-stained sleeves.

"First off, I wasn't asking for your permission. Second, why were you thrown in prison? How do we know we can trust you? *What is your name?*"

The girl sat down against a tree and sighed. "I lived in Ash—in another village before I came here, to the Southern Tribe. My whole village was—" She seemed to be contemplating what to say. "I had to leave my village. I had to find somewhere else. This was the first civilization I had seen so far, so I slipped past the guards and tried to make a living. I stole what I need, maybe a little bit more, and that's why those guards were yelling at me."

"Can we trust you?" I repeated.

The girl shrugged. "That's entirely up to you. I just wanted to get out of there."

"You didn't answer my question!" I fumed.

"What—" the girl began, but Sonny stepped between us, crouching down so he was eye-level with the girl.

"What do they call you, madam?" he asked, lending her his hand like he was inviting her to dance.

"Amber Leaf, though my friends called me Sparky," the girl said, taking Sonny's hand.

Sonny pulled Amber Leaf to her feet and began twirling her around in a rhythmic dance. "'Amber Leaf' suits you."

When Amber Leaf said 'Sparky', Flame Fall's eyes widened and he blinked, staring at his shoes. I met his gaze and we had a silent conversation that went something like this:

Me: *You okay?*

Him: *Wha?*

Me: *You acted weird when she said 'Sparky'.*

Him: *I'll tell you later.*

Me: *Okay.*

Flame Fall gave me an 'I'm-going-to-say-I'm-fine-but-I'm-really-not' smile.

Sonny and Amber Leaf concluded their dance and I climbed

back onto his horse. "We should get going."

News flash: When Amber Leaf looks at you, you are afraid to do *everything*. Her amber eyes seemed to freeze me in place.

"Okay. Where are we going?" she asked everyone.

Everyone shrugged.

We started back on our trail to nowhere again, and Oak River pulled his horse up to mine. "I might have an idea for how to find Dakota."

I looked at him with surprise. "How?"

"If she was taken in her dreams, maybe that's how we find her."

"Really?"

"It makes sense."

"Yeah, it does," I agreed. "Good thinking, Oak River. I hope you're up for it because you're the one trying it."

Chapter 20

Dakota

I stood in the center of the cavern, a translucent sword in my hand.

For the past two hours, the magical cave had been generating holographic enemies for me to fight. Only the sword I held in my hand could defeat them, but if I tried to kick or hit them, my limb would go right through them. They were a variety of things: wolves, giant hawks, demons, heavily armed villagers, and even rabid squirrels.

Sweat dripped down my forehead and soaked through my shirt. The cavern had cleaned my clothes, but I had left off my sleeveless jacket.

I swung my sword at an advancing wolf, whose dark coat reminded me of Astraea. I gasped when the wolf launched itself at me, its ghostly maw stretched wide.

I rolled aside and stabbed the wolf in the stomach. The animal dissolved into mist and disappeared. I heard something behind me and whipped around swinging my sword over my head. Shock jolted through my body as my blade hit another, solid one. I looked up and saw Black Raven looking at me, his beige eyes seeming to pierce my soul.

"Can I—" I withdrew my sword and swung the blade at his neck. "—help you?"

116

Black Raven slammed his sword into mine, blocking my blow. He forced my sword backwards towards me, but I immediately moved my blade from under his and kicked out my foot, catching him in the stomach.

He grunted in pain for a millisecond then swung at me. "No I—" I ducked. "—just wanted to test you; see how your fighting skills are."

I seized his sword arm, pulled him closer to me, and elbowed him hard in the nose. He groaned in pain, and I watched with satisfaction as blood flowed from his nostrils. As he lifted his left hand up to his nose, I dove the hilt of my sword into the crook of his elbow. Black Raven let out a whimper of agony.

I grabbed his sword from his fingers and soon I had Black Raven trapped; his blade pressed against the back of his neck, and my sword tip angled at his windpipe.

"You're an amazing swordsman," Black Raven admitted. "But you need improvement."

Something sharp poked my side and I looked down and saw Black Raven had a small dagger readied to jab into my side.

"I wouldn't do that," I warned. Before Black Raven could process what I said, I drove my sword hilt as hard as I could into his wrist. I heard a small *crack*, and a *pop*, and Black Raven gasped in pain. His dagger clattered to the ground. "I wouldn't do that," I repeated, kicking his dagger across the cave floor.

"Do you surrender?" I asked.

Black Raven chuckled lightheartedly. "I like your guts."

My sword tip touched Black Raven's neck. "Surrender or die," I said.

"Fine, fine." Black Raven held up his hands.

I smiled. "Cool. But I get to kick you one more time." I lashed out with my foot, catching Black Raven in the groin. "You definitely deserved that one."

Black Raven writhed in pain on the floor for a moment before stumbling to his feet and forcing a pained smile across his face. "You're better than I expected, Dakota."

"Yeah, yeah," I dropped the swords, the cave morphing back into my home. I walked over to the kitchen and took a boiling kettle off of the stove. "Tea?"

Black Raven chuckled and sat down on the couch, warming his hands by the fire. "That would be nice."

"Speaking of nice," I began as I took two cups from the cupboard. "Why are you so decent all of a sudden? When I first came here, you acted like I was an annoying little pest." I handed him his tea, sitting on a chair across from him.

Black Raven laughed, suddenly interested in his tea.

Is he blushing?

"Well, I didn't really know how beau—how annoying you'd be, but now you're just *there*; you don't have a good purpose—"

"Thanks," I muttered as I sipped my tea. He was definitely blushing.

"—and you don't have a bad aura, so I don't really know what to do with you."

"Thanks," I repeated, standing. I set my tea down. "I'm going to change into some non-sweaty clothes. I'll be right back."

Black Raven nodded, looking slightly relieved. "That's fine."

I went into my room and closed the door, finding a dark green and blue dress laid out on my bed. I looked at the wall. "Really? You expect me to wear *that*?"

Thankfully, the wall didn't reply, but a glowing pink orb materialized in front of me. "Well, he's obviously into you."

My eyes widened. "Who—what are you?"

"Dakota, I am the soul of this cave. My name is

Mareeninkinusmolia," the orb dipped.

"Um can—" I began.

"Just call me M.K. I'm fine with it." M.K. glowed brightly. "Right, so the dress—"

"Oh no. I will not wear *that*!" I folded my arms.

M.K. sighed and circled my body, bobbing up and down. "Fine, fine. How about *this*?" The green and blue dress disappeared, replaced by a flowy green dress with silver swirls weaving through it.

I had to admit, it *was* kind of pretty. I sighed and began to take off my clothes, but M.K. stopped me. "You're going to take too long. Let me help." A warm pink light surrounded me and in a split second, my clothes were replaced with the silver and green dress. My bun had fallen out, so my dark hair fell down my shoulders in waves.

M.K. glowed happily. "Well, get out there! He won't wait forever!"

I sighed and walked towards the door. When I went into the living room, Black Raven was staring intently at the flames, taking small glances as I walked over.

I sat down in the chair and sipped my cold tea, watching Black Raven's eyes examine my outfit. "Nice dress," he commented.

I looked down at my bare feet, suddenly interested in my toes. "So, is there anything else you want?" I stood, ready to take my teacup to the kitchen.

"Yes."

I looked up and met Black Raven's beige eyes. "And what is that?" My palms turned sweaty and I clamped my fingers over the cup to keep them from shaking.

Black Raven stood and walked over to me. He pushed a piece of hair from my face. He took the teacup from my hands and placed it on the table behind him. "I don't know how to phrase this."

I took up his hands in mine, which were just as shaky as my own. My breath trembled as I heaved a sigh.

Black Raven, I realized, was too nervous to make a move, so I'd have to do it myself. I pulled him closer to me and kissed him. I compared this kiss to the one me and Oak River had shared. This one wasn't like Oak River's; this one felt *real*. I pulled away after a moment and shock ran through me.

I became aware of Oak River standing in the shadows of the hallway, peeking through the doorway at us. Black Raven's back was to him, so he hadn't seen Oak River.

"I'm going to get some rest," I said, switching my gaze to Black Raven, putting on a charming smile. "See you later."

Black Raven smiled and nodded, and I guided him towards the door. Only once his footsteps receded in the echoey hallway did I go into my room and slam the door behind me, turning on Oak River. "What are you doing here?"

Oak River stared at me in shock.

"I came to rescue you, but—" he whispered. "—*What was that?*"

I pushed past him and began rummaging through my trunk at the foot of my bed. I found a pair of fluffy pants and tossed them onto my bed.

"'That' is none of your business. Now answer my question." I turned around and looked into Oak River's innocent green eyes for a moment, immediately searching through my trunk again. I couldn't bear to look into his eyes; it was too much to have me knowing that we were cousins, but not him.

I found a silky dark green shirt and tossed that onto my bed. I heard Oak River sigh, "Dakota, look at me, please!"

I spun around and placed my hands on my hips. "What do you want me to say, Oak River? We didn't exactly part on good terms, and certain events have just made things—awkward between us. I'm sorry."

Oak River's eyes widened and he took my hand. "Dakota, what, what events? What are you talking about? Wha—"

I scoffed and pulled my hand away. "You're right; what am I apologizing for? We never were a couple, so—"

"Violet Heart has left, so we have no obstacles to block our way—"

Anger boiled in my chest. "No! Oak River the only obstacle in the way of our *relationship*—" I had to spit out the last word. "—is *you*! You are the only thing in the way of our happiness. You and Violet Heart had an affair. *You* beat up Sonny, and even though I think he's a pest sometimes, that doesn't make beating him up right!" My eyes moistened. "I really don't need you in my life right now!"

Oak River's eyes widened. "What has gotten into you?!"

I sobbed, "You," and threw my fist into Oak River's stomach, but instead of it hitting flesh, it went through Oak River's body like I had punched water. Oak River shouted something at me, but it was indistinguishable as he started to dissolve like mist. His green eyes stared at me with shocked, angry disbelief. When he disappeared, I fainted and shook my head.

I changed into my clothes and hurled my dress at the wall. Before the fabric hit the wall, M.K. appeared out of nowhere and stopped the dress, magically unfolding it and smoothing out all the wrinkles. M.K. glowed a dark red. "Two things: don't ever throw my gifts again; and you are going back!"

"You can't send me back!" I scoffed.

"Try me, Dakota," M.K. challenged, glowing bright blue. "I'll do it!"

"Fine, whatever."

"Two more things: I made a travelling pack that can

produce any food you want—" a leather satchel appeared around my shoulder, and the green and silver dress folded itself and slipped into my bag. "—and two," M.K. continued. "You might not get there for a couple of hours, so it'll probably feel like you're in some sort of hyper sleep."

I furrowed my eyebrows. "But—"

"Good luck!" M.K. said, and the world around me crumbled into darkness.

Chapter 21

Sonny

I really don't know what to make of Amber Leaf; she's cute, resourceful, and smart. But I don't know if we can trust her.

Like Moon Song might have mentioned before, when Amber Leaf looks at you, it pins you to the spot. She wasn't that talkative around the others, but she seemed plenty okay with talking to me.

It had been a day since we left the Southern Tribe. Oak River had attempted to contact Dakota, but refused to talk about anything that happened. We rode near the back of the group, and I watched Oak River and Moon Song talk a little ways away.

"Why does that girl hate me?" Amber Leaf asked from behind me. *Probably because she doesn't trust you.* I shrugged.

"Who is the guy she's talking to?"

"Um—" I began.

"Does that girl even *have* a boyfriend? Is that him? They look too similar to me to be a couple. Are—"

I yanked on the horse's lead, causing us to stop. "Stop talking! I know I might be a chatterbox sometimes, but now I feel sorry that my peers have to live with me. We don't even know if we can *trust* you!" I spurred my horse back into motion.

Amber Leaf's eyes widened, then she dropped her head. "You're right. Maybe I should just leave you guys." She slung her crossbow over her back and started sliding off of the horse. I seized her wrist and pulled her back on.

"You might be annoying as ever, but I'm not so cold-hearted as to let a small girl such as yourself go out in the forest in the middle of winter with no food."

Amber Leaf took an apple from inside her shirt. "I have food!"

I smiled and looked forward. Moon Song was looking at me. With her silver eyes, she was almost as terrifying as Amber Leaf. Moon Song looked at Amber Leaf, then at me, then back at Amber Leaf.

I shook my head. *It's not like that!*

Moon Song blinked and turned away from me.

Silver! I wanted to shout, *I don't like her.*

Moon Song didn't talk to me for a while, and when she finally did it was to ask me if I had any spare cloth to wrap a cut on her arm. When I said no, Moon Song gave me that 'I-hate-you' glare and started talking to Flame Fall.

I started to push the horse to go faster, but Amber Leaf put her hand on my shoulder, stopping me. "Do you hear that?" she asked.

I was about to protest when I heard it: a soft, *whooshing* sound, like something small hurtling through the air.

"Ready your guard!" I shouted at the others, turning my horse around. Oak River paused to listen for a second, then drew his sword and spurred his horse to my side, followed by the others. Soon we had formed a circle with our horses, facing outwards. Everyone had swords ready, and Amber Leaf's pupils had narrowed so they looked almost feline. Weird.

We all searched in different directions for the attackers, and suddenly Moon Song shouted, "There!"

I spun my horse around to see where she was pointing and saw something whisking through the air towards us. As 'something' neared us, I realized it was a long, pointed icicle flying towards us like a possessed wintry sword of death.

The icicle flew straight towards me, and I was frozen (no pun intended) with shock.

"Sonny!" Moon Song screamed, but I barely heard it. The icicle was one hundred feet from us now. Fifty. Twenty. Ten.

Suddenly, Oak River hit the ice with a *crack* and the icicle shattered in half. The back half flew over my shoulder, making Moon Song let out a strangled gasp, but the front, pointy half was still determined to kill me. I barely heard my girlfriend's gasp.

Just as I thought the icicle would fly right through me, someone shoved my shoulder and I fell sideways off my horse, landing hard on my side. A wave of sharp pain went through my half-healed arm. I heard my horse whinny and the clomping of hooves as my horse galloped away through the trees in a white blur.

I groaned and got to my feet. Moon Song and Oak River had gathered around me. I thought it was considerate for them to care so much around me, but then I looked down at my feet, and both bile and sobs rose in my throat.

Flame Fall laid on the ground, his swords still clenched in his hands. Blood pooled around Flame Fall's back, and from his stomach protruded the long, thin icicle.

A loud scream of rage escaped my mouth and I fell to my knees. I grabbed my brother's shoulders and shook him vigorously. "Flame Fall!"

Flame Fall's eyes were dimming, the light leaving them. "Sonny—" he dropped one of his swords and put his hand on mine. "—I'll be here always."

Tears streamed down my face. "NO!" I screamed at the top of my lungs. "Flame Fall, please don't do this! You're the last family I have left!"

Flame Fall weakly raised his other hand and pointed at Moon Song, then his hand went limp and fell into the pool of blood, splattering my clothes.

"No. No! No!" I shook Flame Fall, but his eyes were lifeless, his body limp.

Tears fell from my face, mixing with Flame Fall's blood. Even though I knew he was gone, I screamed at him to come back for several minutes. Finally, I dropped my head and let the tears fall into my lap. I felt a hand on my shoulder. Moon Song sat beside me, her silver eyes flicking back and forth between me and my brother's dead body.

I turned and pulled her into an embrace, and she didn't say anything, just let me cry into her chest. She rubbed my head the way Flame Fall used to and kissed my forehead. Everything was silent.

Suddenly, Flame Fall's body started glowing. I sat straight up and watched in amazement. A translucent figure rose from the body, and I realized that the figure *was* my brother; his soul.

But the Flame Fall that floated in front of me was in much better condition: his wounds were gone, his face happy and glowing.

Flame Fall's soul floated past me and began morphing into something with dark brown fur, a strong maw, and an elegant, fluffy tail. A wolf. A solid, not translucent wolf. Around his front left ankle, the fur was golden. Weird.

I heard a rustle in the undergrowth behind me, and a familiar brown she-wolf trotted to my brother's body, her hazel eyes glowing.

Astraea bent over Flame Fall's body and sniffed his chest. The wolf Flame Fall walked to Astraea's side and carefully, using his teeth, ripped open the front my dead brother's shirt. Underneath the fabric, hanging around a leather cord, was a beautiful golden wedding ring.

'Wolfie' cautiously ripped the leather cord and lifted it so that Astraea could see the gold band. Astraea's eyes widened and she froze.

Wolfie's ears gradually fell flat against his skull, and his tail fell to the ground, but his brown eyes remained fixed on Astraea.

Finally, after a moment of silence, Astraea licked Wolfie's cheek and barked softly.

The ring vanished from the cord and the fur around Astraea's front left ankle turned golden. Wolfie's eyes brightened and he and Astraea bounded into the forest, stopping once to quickly glance back at us.

I tried to keep my gaze from Flame Fall's body, but my eyes refused. My brother's eyes, once full of life and light, were now shattered and dull. Choking down a sob, I got to my feet and brushed Moon Song's hand off my shoulder. "I need to be alone."

Moon Song nodded. "We'll wait here, but—"

"Don't take too long, okay?" Oak River said, looking around cautiously.

Moon Song kissed my cheek and briefly squeezed my hand. "Take as long as you need," she whispered into my ear. I nodded and turned, sprinting away into the woods.

I thought being alone would help me calm myself, but as soon as I ran away from Moon Song, tears streamed down my face again. They made my sight blurry, but I could still tell where the trees were and the ground sloped. I skidded to a halt in a clearing, snow coating the ground.

I bent over and put my hands on my knees, panting. I wiped my eyes with the heel of my palm and straightened my back, my eyes falling on something in the snow. My heart seemed to stop when I saw it.

A body.

The eyes were closed, thankfully, because I was already on the verge of wetting my pants. The lips were blue, and the dark hair was fanned out around the head. The only sign that the person was alive was the faint cloud of steam coming from the mouth as small breaths were let in and out. The scariest thing out of all of this was that I recognized that face and the emerald green necklace sparkling on her chest—Dakota.

Chapter 22

Moon Song

As soon as Sonny disappeared into the woods, I heard the *thump, thumping* of horse hooves nearing us. Hawk Feather was coming.

"Get into the tree," Oak River told me.

"What about you?" I asked, starting towards the nearest oak tree. "What—"

"Don't worry about me." Oak River pushed me into the bough and ducked into an elder bush. I sighed and climbed higher until I was completely submerged in the trees branches, but I had a clear view of the forest floor.

Hawk Feather appeared on a horse right next to the tree I was in, closely followed by Dawn Whisper, Lion Claw, and the white girl. I gaped at the white girl's magnificent white cloak, which was neatly draped over her horse's back. Her red hair was swept over one shoulder, and I swear she kept glancing at the elder bush where my brother was hiding. If I had to, I would jump down and impale the alien with my knives, but only if it was an emergency.

Lion Claw looked down at the bodies, frowning with false sorrow. "A runaway and the street rat."

Something Sonny wasn't quite aware of yet: the back half

of the flying icicle had killed Amber Leaf. I hated Amber Leaf before, but now, looking at her black hair fanned out around her head, her sharp, amber eyes empty and lifeless, and the blood stained snow around her, I felt guilt wrapping around my chest, weighing me down like a stone.

Lion Claw jumped down from his horse and kicked red snow onto Amber Leaf's lifeless face. "I guess they both deserved it."

The white girl's face was grim. "The horses are still here, so the others must be close. Hawk Feather and Lion Claw, check northeast. Dawn Whisper, check northwest. I'll secure their horses and check this area."

Dawn Whisper started northwest, then paused. "Ginger Bloom, what makes you think you can survive out here on your own?"

Ginger Bloom furrowed her eyebrows. "Just because I'm the chief's daughter doesn't mean I can't fight!"

Dawn Whisper rolled her eyes and spurred her horse away. Hawk Feather and Lion Claw both gave Ginger Bloom doubtful looks then galloped away.

Once the sound of hooves faded, Ginger Bloom dismounted her horse and approached Amber Leaf's body. Using two fingers, she closed the girl's eyes. Ginger Bloom did the same to Flame Fall before standing up and looking directly at the elder bush. "You can come out now. I won't hurt you without provocation."

Oak River stood and dusted snow off his clothes. "Ginger Bloom, is it?"

Ginger Bloom nodded. "Where are the others?"

I shifted slightly, ready to jump down from the tree. Oak River's hand unfolded, his fingers spread wide in a familiar gesture: stop.

I huffed and continued watching.

Ginger Bloom sighed. "Why did you come?"

"I thought you already knew that." Oak River cracked his knuckles.

Ginger Bloom eyed Oak River's muscular biceps, not with admiration, but with fear. "I—I do, but I wanted to hear it from you."

Oak River narrowed his eyes. "Why? You already heard it from Sonny and Moon Song."

Ginger Bloom folded her arms in front of her chest. "I want to know, Oak River! And if you have any brains in that in head of yours, you'll tell me!"

Oak River's muscles tensed. "Fight me."

Ginger Bloom undid her cloak and draped it over her horse's back, revealing a white bodysuit. She unsheathed two knives that were strapped to her thighs and threw one at Oak River, who was backed against my tree. The knife skimmed Oak River's neck and impaled itself in the brown bark.

"So be it," Oak River growled, baring his swords. He launched himself at Ginger Bloom, who ducked to the side and grabbed his wrist, twisting his arm around. Oak River gasped with pain, sweeping his leg behind him and catching Ginger Bloom in the ankle. She fell into the snow, her red hair vibrant against the ground.

I brought my head forward, ready to leap down and help, but something tugged my hair. I reached up a hand and discovered that my hair had wrapped itself—somehow— around a tree branch. Great!

Oak River slipped his arms out of Ginger Bloom's grip and spun around. In one swift movement, he had pinned her down; one knee was on her chest, her arm trapped under his shin, and his other knee was pinning her other arm down. He placed his hands on either side of her head and leaned down closer to her face.

"I beat you, now what?" he asked.

Ginger Bloom panted. "Honestly?"

"Honestly."

"I decide whether to kick your groin or politely ask you to get off." Ginger Bloom's teal eyes sparkled. "I've made my decision. Please get off."

"Give me your knife."

"Fine." Ginger Bloom wrenched her arm from under Oak River's leg and stuck her knife in the snow. "Get off me."

Oak River stood and picked up her knife. He stared at it for a second, then tucked it into his boot. He lent a hand out to Ginger Bloom.

She grabbed it and he heaved her upright. For a second, she lost her balance and fell forward into my brother. Oak River grabbed her shoulders and steadied her. She looked up at him, and he looked down at her, and I felt some sort of bile churning in my stomach. Perhaps it was the sisterly protectiveness, or maybe the sight of Flame Fall's body still made my insides turn. I don't know.

I yanked my hair from the tree branch and (gracefully) leapt down from the tree, landing right next to the two, crouching. Both stared at me with surprise, and Oak River looked like he had forgotten I was there. I stood up.

"Would you two stop goggling at each other so we can get a move on?" I asked, brushing tree dust from my pants.

"Is this your—*girlfriend?*" Ginger Bloom asked.

Oak River's eyes widened. "What—"

The elder bush behind us rustled and Sonny fell into the snow, painting. "No—she's—my girlfriend. No one else's—Oak River—is her—brother."

Ginger Bloom looked back and forth between us. "Oh."

My eyes widened as Sonny grabbed my hand. "You guys need to see this!"

He yanked me back the way he came, not pausing to wait for Oak River. He wound around the trees and we finally emerged into a snowy clearing. Lying in the center was a body.

My breath caught in my throat. "Dakota."

Sonny nodded. "She's barely breathing."

I ran to Dakota's side, knelt in the snow and opened my satchel (which Hawk Feather didn't take from me) and rummaged through the contents. Nothing in there would help, so I shut my satchel and grabbed Dakota's hands. The skin was as cold as ice.

"We need to get her out of the snow," I told Sonny.

Oak River and Ginger Bloom burst from the forest. My brother's face was slack with shock. "Dakota."

"Is *she* your girlfriend?" Ginger Bloom asked.

"Um—" Oak River began.

"No," I answered firmly.

Sonny fitted his arms underneath Dakota's body and lifted her up, cradling her head in the crook of his elbow. I didn't know he was that strong. (To be honest, I didn't think he had any physical strength, but we learn something new every day.)

Sonny carried Dakota out of the clearing, looking for a decent place to set her down. Finally, he found a not so snowy patch of land underneath a thick-leafed tree. He laid her down, resting her head against a root that protruded from the ground.

"We need to warm her up!" I said.

Oak River unlaced his jacket and wrapped it around Dakota's shoulders. He took up Dakota's hand in his and squeezed.

Ginger Bloom eyed Oak River. Her teal eyes darted back and forth between him and Dakota. "Will she live?"

"I don't know," I admitted.

With his other hand, Oak River grabbed Dakota's shoulder and shook it. "Dakota wake up! Please! Wake up!" I looked at Dakota's face.

Silence. The only thing that we could hear was the light wind that whistled through the tree branches.

Then, suddenly, Dakota shuddered. Her teal eyes stared at the sky, confusion clouding them. Her breaths came in a steadier pattern, and once she realized she was holding Oak River's hand, she let go.

She took a shaky breath. "Hey guys."

Chapter 23

Dakota

It seemed like just a couple of minutes had passed since M.K. sent me here, but when I woke up, my body ached like I had been asleep for hours.

I pushed myself upright and pushed Oak River's jacket from my shoulders, handing it to him. "You need to keep warm too."

Oak River looked at me, disappointment and confusion in his green eyes. A girl stood behind him, more alien-looking than any person I've met. She had pale skin that was slightly darker than the snow, and her hair was red like fire.

She had dark teal eyes that eyed me warily. I can't blame her; I was probably almost dead, and I *am* pretty intimidating.

"W—What happened?" I stammered. I looked around and didn't see Flame Fall. "W—Where's Flame Fall? Who's she, and why is she—*white?*" I looked at the pale girl.

Moon Song wrapped her hand around my shoulders. "We can discuss that later. For now, let's see if we can get you in a decent health condition." She looked at Oak River. "You go with Ginger Bloom and collect firewood, and food if you get the chance. Me and Sonny will stay with Dakota."

The white girl, Ginger Bloom, nodded and pulled Oak River to his feet. She led the way away into the woods.

After they had gone, Moon Song started going through her satchel. Her eyes widened with shock and she pulled out a blanket, staring at it in awe.

"How does that fit in there?" Sonny asked.

Moon Song shrugged and wrapped it around my shoulders. "I have no idea."

Sonny smiled a little and wrapped my hands in his. Moon Song put her arm around my shoulders again.

"Thanks, guys," I said. "Sorry that I left."

Moon Song rubbed my shoulder. "It wasn't your fault you got kidnapped."

I nodded. "You're right."

* * *

Oak River and Ginger Bloom returned with two rabbits and a squirrel, which we roasted over a warm fire and ate for dinner. After we finished, everyone settled around the flames to sleep, except for Oak River, who insisted on keeping watch.

I laid down, tucking my arm under my head, and shut my eyes, the scene of Black Raven's kiss continually running through my head.

When I opened them again, I was standing in a room made out of stone, roughly the size of my house. On one side was a four-poster bed, a nightstand, and a desk and chair. On the other side was a dresser and a door.

I felt like this place should be familiar.

The door opened, and Black Raven came in, unaware of my presence. He opened his dresser and searched through it. He grabbed the hem of his black shirt and in one fluid motion, removed it from his body. On his back was an ink drawing of flames dancing across someone's palm. Sparks swirled in a spiral pattern up Black Raven's spine, continuing up his neck and on his shoulders.

Should I speak? I thought, not wanting to break the silence. *What have I got to lose?*

"The ink art on your back is cool," I said quietly. Black Raven spun around, his beige eyes wide.

"Dakota!" he said.

"Hi."

"I thought—Why did you come back?" he asked.

I tilted my head. "I didn't want to. I just went to sleep and woke up here."

The corners of Black Raven's mouth twitched. "Were you thinking about me?"

"What?" My face felt hot. "No."

"You are a terrible liar," Black Raven said, shaking his head.

"Okay, maybe a little," I admitted, "but I didn't know I'd be *here*. In your bedroom."

Black Raven glanced down at his jet necklace. "I wasn't expecting visitors."

"Well I know that!" I said. "I don't think if you knew I was coming that you would come in here half naked. Even if you did, I would *not* be distracted by your abs and beautiful ink art—"

"It's called a tattoo," Black Raven said, smiling. "I have a question."

"Yeah?" I walked over to Black Raven's bed and sat on the edge. The blankets were soft and smelled of eucalyptus leaves.

"Last time I saw you—" He pulled out another black shirt and pulled it on over his head.

"Oh, yeah." My face grew even hotter. "That was—" *What should I say? Great? Awkward?* "Pretty nice."

Black Raven grinned and walked over to me. "Did that kiss mean anything or was it just because you didn't know what else to do?"

I shrugged. "Honestly, I was really nervous. In the past week and a half, I've kissed three boys, and there was something wrong with every kiss except yours. Flame Fall thought I was Astraea and Oak River is—well—my cousin. I thought that if I kissed you, something bad would happen and ruin everything, so—"

"But nothing did. And it was perfect," Black Raven interrupted.

"Yeah. Perfect."

"Another question."

"Ask away," I said. I rubbed my sweaty palms against my pants.

"Could we try that again just to make sure it wasn't an accident?" Black Raven grabbed my hand and pulled me to my feet. He tucked a piece of my hair behind my ear.

I smiled and pressed my lips against his, closing my eyes. He set his hands on my waist, then slowly slipped them around my midsection. I wrapped my arms around his neck, sliding my fingers through his short, soft, black hair. Black Raven walked forward, making me move back, until I felt the edge of the bed against the back of my legs. I pulled away, pressing my forehead to his. "Can I see your—what do you call it? Tattoo?"

Black Raven's beige eyes met mine and he smiled again. "Are you asking me to undress, Dakota?"

"No, I'm just curious," I answered.

Black Raven took off his shirt and we sat on the bed. He turned around, guiding my hands to his waist. I ran my fingers over the flaming hand, the fire, and the sparks. Black Raven turned around again and I saw the sparks stop at his shoulders. I start to take my hands away, but Black Raven grabbed my wrists and placed them on his shoulders. His skin was soft, and I could feel the muscle underneath it. My eyes moved with my hands: his shoulders, his chest, his stomach, and then his jet pendant.

"Do you like it?" Black Raven asked, his eyes still on me.

"You, the tattoo, or the necklace?" I asked, my eyes drifting to his.

"Everything."

I frowned. "I don't know. It's all so disappointing. I thought it would have more of the wow factor," I said teasingly.

Black Raven narrowed his eyes at me, then drove his fingers into my side and began tickling me. I collapsed in a fit of laughter on the bed next to him, pressing my face against the gray blankets. I could hear him laughing on the other side of me. I rolled onto my back, my stomach hurting from laughing so hard. Black Raven continued to tickle me.

Finally he stopped and collapsed next to me. We both sighed. The back of his hand brushed mine, and I shifted my hand and laced my fingers through his.

"I'm not really here, am I?" I asked, staring at the stone ceiling.

"No, which is why I want to enjoy this as long as possible." He rolled onto his side. I did the same. He grabbed my waist and pulled me into a kiss. We laid there, sharing the same breath, smiling, and kissing. Black Raven pulled me closer, and I feel his cold jet necklace against my chest.

He pressed his hand to the side of my face, running his thumb along my jawline. I looked at his face, taking in all of his features: his beige eyes, his perfect nose, his chiseled chin. I noticed he had dimples when he smiled. My eyes rested on his, and Black Raven ran his finger over the scar he gave me when we first met. "I have to tell you something," he said.

"What?" I asked rubbing his hands with mine.

"I'll have to kidnap you again."

I raised an eyebrow and smiled. "Since when has that been a problem?"

"Not just you; your friends too. The demons want you

dead. It'll take a while for you to get there, maybe a couple months, but I could delay your execution."

"How much delay?" I asked.

"Push it out to a year or so," Black Raven replied.

"A *year*?" My eyes widened.

"Yeah, it will give you time to prepare and train for combat. I'll find you the most comfortable lodging I can. The most bedrooms I can get is three, so that might be a little awkward."

"It's better than two."

"Yeah," I agreed. "So when would this happen?"

"Tomorrow."

"Oh." I rolled onto my back and fumbled with my emerald necklace. "I'm probably going to wake up soon, so see you tomorrow."

Black Raven nodded and kissed my cheek. "See you tomorrow."

Chapter 24

Sonny

After Dakota went to sleep, Oak River climbed a tree to get a good view of the forest around us, and Ginger Bloom curled up next to the dying embers of the fire.

I stared at the sky, unable to sleep. Moon Song laid next to me, her hand squeezing mine. I sighed, "Hi."

Moon Song rolled onto her side and kissed my cheek. "Hi." She sat up and got to her feet, pulling me up with her. "Come on."

"What are you doing?" I asked, brushing dirt from my butt. "We can't exactly leave th—"

"We're not leaving," Moon Song said. She grabbed my other hand and put it on her waist, letting her right hand rest on my shoulder. Her silver eyes glistened in the fading sunlight.

Moon Song rested her head on my chest and began swaying as she hummed a pleasant melody. It reminded me of what Mother used to sing to me before I'd go to sleep. I kissed the top of her head and swayed with her.

"I love you, you know that?" Moon Song asked.

I removed my hand from her waist and lifted her chin up to face me. I leaned down and kissed her on the lips. She wrapped her hands around my neck and kissed me back. I felt her fingers on my shoulders, then up my neck, and through my hair. I smiled and kissed her again, putting my arms around her waist. I pulled away, pressing my forehead against Moon Song's. "I love you too."

For a long time before we went to sleep, we kissed and swayed to Moon Song's melody.

* * *

In the morning, Dakota was more happy than usual. She kept bouncing on the balls of her feet; constantly smiling at everyone.

"Did you sleep well last night?" Moon Song laughed.

"Excellent!" Dakota answered. Her teal eyes glistened in the winter sun, the light breeze whipping her hair into her face. "You guys should watch out for smoky black tendrils."

I raised an eyebrow and shoved my hands into my armpits to keep them warm. Moon Song and Dakota walked behind me talking.

"So, you never answered my question last night," Dakota said, her voice grim.

"What—?" Moon Song paused. "Oh." She lowered her voice, but I could still hear it. "Flame Fall died last night."

"What? How?"

"A magical flying icicle hit him. But he died heroically; he jumped in front of Sonny and took the hit," Moon Song replied.

"Oh." Dakota and Moon Song walked in silence for a while and I trudged ahead, tears stinging my eyes. Oak River and Ginger Bloom walked in front of me, playfully shoving each other. I smiled, remembering that Violet Heart and I used to do that too.

Moon Song appeared at my side and she slipped her hand

into mine. I smiled and ran my thumb over the back of her hand. "At least we have us, right?"

I nodded, blinking tears from my eyes. "Yeah."

Moon Song stood up on her tiptoes. (I'm so tall I love it), and kissed me on the cheek. Warmth spread through my face with surprising speed. I slowed us down and let Dakota walk in front of us. I pushed Moon Song behind me and crouched down.

"W-What are you doing?" she asked through chattering teeth.

I reached my arms behind me and grabbed her waist, pulling her onto my back. Her arms wrapped around my neck and I stood. "It's called a piggyback ride."

Moon Song didn't protest as we started after the others. Suddenly, Ginger Bloom screamed and fell over.

Moon Song jumped from my back and ran to Ginger Bloom's side. I ran after her. Ginger Bloom shrieked as black smoky tendrils wrapped around her body. Oak River gasped and spun around, his green eyes widening as he saw something behind my back.

I turned around and saw a mass of darkness flying towards us. I drew Tiny. "Get Ginger Bloom out!" I told Oak River.

Oak River nodded and disappeared behind me. Moon Song grunted, "It's not working, I—"

Her voice was cut off by a scream of terror.

I turned around, my sword ready, only to see that the tendrils had wrapped around Moon Song's feet. She tried to walk towards me, but her feet were rooted to the spot; she fell into my chest. I dropped Tiny and wrapped my arms around her, watching with horror as the tendrils engulfed Oak River and Dakota. Dakota looked way too calm for my liking: her face was calm, her eyes met mine and she seemed to say *It's fine. Everything will be fine.*

I wanted to scream that she doesn't know that, but

I looked down into Moon Song's terrified gaze and kissed her forehead. "I love you no matter what happens," I told her.

Tears welled in Moon Song's eyes as she shook her head, craning her head up to kiss me. I closed my eyes, shutting out everything around me as the smoky tendrils curled around my torso, my neck, and finally my face, causing the world around me to go black.

*Once there was a young girl who learned a shocking truth about her best friend. The demons began to **Unfold** from there. They left, only to **Return** for her children and their friends to have to face. Now it is time for them to **End**.*

Coming soon: Demons Ending

Sigma's Bookshelf (www.SigmasBookshelf.com) is an independent book publishing company that exclusively publishes the work of teenage authors, who are between the ages of 13 and 19. The company was founded in 2016 by Minnesota teenager Justin M. Anderson, whose first book, *Saving Stripes: A Kitty's Story*, was published when he was 14, and has since sold hundreds of copies.

"I know there are a lot of other teenagers out there who are good writers and deserve to have their work published, but don't have access to the kinds of resources I do. I wanted to help them," he said.

Sigma's Bookshelf is a sponsored project of Springboard for the Arts, a nonprofit arts service organization. Contributions on behalf of Sigma's Bookshelf may be made payable to Springboard for the Arts and are tax deductible to the extent permitted by law. Donations can be made online at www.SigmasBookshelf.com/donate.